Praise for Charles Baxter's

# *There's Something I Want You to Do*

"Few writers, if any, are as capable of pursuing such an inevitable truth as this—and in so graceful, subdued, and artful a manner—as Charles Baxter."
                                    —*The Philadelphia Inquirer*

"[*There's Something I Want You to Do*'s] characters slip in and out of one another's stories, and while some never meet, they eventually constitute . . . a shimmering web of interconnectedness."
                                    —*The New York Times Book Review*

"Nearly as organic as a novel, [*There's Something I Want You to Do*] is more intriguing, more fun in disclosing its connective tissues through tales that stand well on their own."          —*Kirkus Reviews* (starred review)

"Baxter creates empathetic and nuanced portraits of human nature. . . . Reminds us that happiness, like morality, is fluid and that we must guard it accordingly."
                                    —*Miami Herald*

"A master of the form contemplates the abhorrent and admirable choices we make and what finally leads a person to choose the high road."
                                    —*O, The Oprah Magazine*

"An explosive addition to [Baxter's] already stellar resume."

—*Den of Geek!* ("The Must-Read Fiction of 2015")

"Baxter's writing is sharper than ever."

—*The Gazette* (Cedar Rapids, Iowa)

"Will make readers hungry for more."

—*Library Journal* (starred review)

"Baxter's writing is characterized by . . . unselfconsciousness [and] artless clarity. His characters take on their own lives. They subsist so independently of their creator that we almost forget that there is a creator."

—*The Rumpus*

"With his latest collection, Charles Baxter has given us something altogether new in contemporary fiction: a series of moral tales that contain zero moralizing. . . . Here is a cast of characters unparalleled since Sherwood Anderson's *The Book of the Grotesque*, with a modern-day Minneapolis as tangible and strange as his Winesburg, Ohio."       —Jamie Quatro, author of *I Want to Show You More*

"[Baxter's] prose resonates with distinctive turns of phrase that capture human ambiguity and uncertainty: trouble waits patiently at home, irony is the new chastity, and a dying man lives in the house that pain designed for him." —*Publishers Weekly* (starred review)

Charles Baxter

# There's Something I Want You to Do

Charles Baxter is the author of the novels *The Feast of Love* (a finalist for the National Book Award), *The Soul Thief*, *Saul and Patsy*, *Shadow Play*, and *First Light*, and the story collections *Gryphon*, *Believers*, *A Relative Stranger*, *Through the Safety Net*, and *Harmony of the World*. The stories "Bravery" and "Charity," which appear in *There's Something I Want You to Do*, were included in *The Best American Short Stories*. Baxter lives in Minneapolis and teaches at the University of Minnesota and in the MFA Program for Writers at Warren Wilson College.

www.charlesbaxter.com

*There's
Something
I Want You
to Do*

# There's Something I Want You to Do

### STORIES

*Charles Baxter*

For Lenore Hirsch,
with all good wishes
from Napa—

Charlie Baxter

August 2, 2012
Napa

VINTAGE CONTEMPORARIES

Vintage Books

A Division of Penguin Random House LLC

New York

FIRST VINTAGE CONTEMPORARIES EDITION, FEBRUARY 2016

Selected stories first appeared in the following: "Avarice" in *Virginia Quarterly
Review* (January 2015); "Bravery" in *Tin House* 54 (Winter 2012) and subsequently
in *The Best American Short Stories 2013*, edited by Elizabeth Strout with Heidi
Pitlor (New York: Houghton Mifflin Harcourt, 2013); "Forbearance" in *Michigan
Quarterly Review* 52, no. 2 (Spring 2013); "Charity" in *McSweeney's*, issue #43 (April
2013) and subsequently in *The Best American Short Stories 2014*, edited by Jennifer
Egan with Heidi Pitlor (New York: Houghton Mifflin Harcourt, 2014); "Loyalty"
in *Harper's* (May 2013); "Chastity" in *The Kenyon Review* (Winter 2014); and "Sloth"
in *New England Review* 34, nos. 3–4 (Winter 2014).

Grateful acknowledgment is made to New Directions Publishing Corp. for
permission to reprint an excerpt from "Seurat's Sunday Afternoon Along the
Seine" by Delmore Schwartz, from *Selected Poems*, copyright © 1959 by Delmore
Schwartz. Reprinted by permission of New Directions Publishing Corp.

The Library of Congress has cataloged the Pantheon edition as follows:
Baxter, Charles, 1947–
[Short stories. Selections]
There's something I want you to do : stories / Charles Baxter.
pages ; cm
I. Baxter, Charles, 1947.    II. Title.
PS3552.A854A6 2014    813'.54—dc23    2014003352

**Vintage Books Trade Paperback ISBN: 978-0-8041-7273-8**
**ebook ISBN: 978-1-101-87002-0**

www.vintagebooks.com

Printed in the United States of America
10   9   8   7   6   5   4   3

*For Daniel and Hannah Baxter*
*and for Arturo Steely*

It is common knowledge that nobody is born with a decalogue already formed, but that everyone builds his own either during his life or at the end, on the basis of his own experiences, or of those of others which can be assimilated to his own; so that everybody's moral universe, suitably interpreted, comes to be identified with the sum of his former experiences, and so represents an abridged form of his biography.

—Primo Levi, *The Reawakening*

# Contents

# PART ONE

# *Bravery*

When she was a teenager, her junior year, her favorite trick involved riding in cars with at least two other girls. You needed a female cluster in there, and you needed to have the plainest one driving. They'd cruise University Avenue in Palo Alto until they spotted some boys together near a street corner. Boys were always ganged up at high-visibility intersections, marking territory and giving off cigarette smoke and musk. At the red light, she'd roll down the window and shout, "Hey, you guys!" The boys would turn toward the car slowly—*very* slowly—trying for cool. Smoke emerged from their faces, from the nose or mouth. "Hey! Do you think we're pretty?" she'd shout. "Do you think we're cute?"

Except for the plain one behind the wheel, the girls she consorted with *were* cute, so the question wasn't really a test. The light would turn green, and they'd speed away before the boys could answer. The pleasure was in seeing them flummoxed. Usually one of the guys, probably the sweetest, or the most eager, would nod and raise his hand to wave. Susan would spy him, the sweet one, through the back window, and she'd smile so that he'd have that smile to hold on to all night. The not-so-sweet good-looking guys just stood there. They were accustomed to being teased, and they always liked it. As for the other boys—well, no one ever cared about them.

Despite what other girls said, boys were not all alike: you

had to make your way through their variables blindly, guessing at hidden qualities, the ones you could live with.

Years later, in college, her roommate said to her, "You always go for the *kind* ones, the *considerate* ones, those types. I mean, where's the fun? I hate those guys. They're so *humane*, and shit like that. Give me a troublemaker any day."

"Yeah, but a troublemaker will give *you* trouble." She was painting her toenails, even though the guys she dated never noticed her toenails. "Trouble comes home. It moves in. It's contagious."

"I can take it. I'm an old-fashioned girl," her roommate said with her complicated irony.

Susan married one of the sweet ones, the kind of man who waved at you. At a San Francisco art gallery on Van Ness, gazing at a painting of a giant pointed index finger with icicles hanging from it, she had felt her concentration jarred when a guy standing next to her said, "Do you smell something?"

He sniffed and glanced up at the ceiling. Metaphor, irony, a come-on? As a pickup line, that one was new to her. In fact, she *had* smelled a slightly rotten-egg scent, so she nodded. "We should get out of here," he said, gesturing toward the door, past the table with the wineglasses and the sign-in book. "It's a gas leak. Before the explosion."

"But maybe it's the paintings," she said.

"The paintings? Giving off explosive gas? That's an odd theory."

"Could be. Part of the modernist assault on the audience?"

He shrugged. "Well, it's rotten eggs or natural gas, one of the two. I don't like the odds. Let's leave."

On the way out, he introduced himself as Elijah, and she laughed and spilled some white wine (she had forgotten she was holding a glass of it) onto her dress just above the hemline. He handed her a monogrammed handkerchief that he had pulled out of some pocket or other, and the first letter on it was *E*, so he probably was an Elijah after all. A monogrammed handkerchief! Maybe he had money. "Here," he said. "Go ahead. Sop it up." He hadn't tried to press his advantage by touching the handkerchief against the dress; he just handed it over, and she pretended to use it to soak up the wine. With the pedestrians passing by and an overhead neon sign audibly humming, he gave off a blue-eyed air of benevolence, but he also looked on guard, hypervigilant, as if he were an ex-Marine. God knows where he had found the benevolence, or where any man ever found it.

"Elijah." She looked at him. In the distance a car honked. The evening sky contained suggestions of rain. His smile persisted: a sturdy street-corner boy turned into a handsome pensive man but very solid-seeming, one thumb inside a belt loop, with a streetlamp behind him giving him an incandescent aura. Physically, he had the frame of a gym rat. She had the odd thought that his skin might taste of sugar, his smile was so kind. Kindness had always attracted her. It made her weak in the knees. "Elijah the prophet? Who answers all questions at the end of time? That one? Your parents must have been religious or something."

"Yeah," he said noncommittally, bored by the topic. "'Or

something' was exactly what they were. They liked to loiter around in the Old Testament. They trusted it. They were farmers, and they believed in catastrophes. But when you have to explain your own name, you . . . well, this isn't a rewarding conversation, is it?" He had a particularly deliberate way of speaking that made him sound as if he had thought up his sentences several minutes ago and was only now getting around to saying them.

She coughed. "So what do you do, Elijah?"

"Oh, that comes later," he said. "Occupations come later. First tell me *your* name."

"Susan," she said. "So much for the introductions." She leaned forward, showing off her great smile. "This wine. It's so bad. I'm kind of glad I spilled it. Shall I spill more of it?" She hadn't had more than a sip, but she felt seriously drunk.

"Well, you could spill it here." He reversed his index finger and lifted up his necktie. "Or there." He pointed at the sidewalk.

"But it's white wine. White wine doesn't really stain." She threw the wineglass into the gutter, where it shattered.

Twenty minutes later, in a coffee shop down by the Embarcadero, she learned that he was a pediatric resident with a particular interest in mitochondrial disorders. Now she understood: out on the street, he had looked at her the way a doctor looks at a child. She herself was a psychiatric social worker, with a job waiting for her at an outpatient clinic in Millbrae. She and Elijah exchanged phone numbers. That night, rattled by their encounter, she couldn't sleep. Three days later, still rattled, she called him and proposed a date, something her mother had advised her never to do with a man. They went to dinner and a movie, and Elijah fell asleep during the previews and didn't wake up for another hour—poor guy, he was so worn out from his work. She didn't bother to explain the plot: a villain had threatened the end of the world—the usual. Elijah was too tired to care.

He didn't warm up to her convincingly—not as she really hoped he would—for a month, until he heard her sing in a local choir, a program that included the Vaughan Williams *Mass in G Minor.* She had a solo in the opening measures of the Benedictus, and when Elijah found her at the reception afterward, his face, as he looked at her, was softened for the first time with actual love, the real thing, that yearning, both hungry and quizzical.

"Your voice. Wow. I was undone," he said, taking a sip of the church-basement coffee, his voice thick. *Undone.* He had a collection of unusual adjectives like that. *Devoted* was another. And *committed.* He used that adjective all the time. Never before had she ever met a man who was comfortable with that particular adjective.

A few months after they were married, they took a trip to Prague. The plan was to get pregnant there amid the European bric-a-brac. On the flight over the Atlantic, he held her hand when the Airbus hit some turbulence. In the seats next to theirs, another young couple sat together, and as the plane lurched, the woman fanned her face with a magazine while the man read passages aloud from the Psalms. "'A thousand shall fall at thy side and ten thousand by thy right hand,'" he read. When the plane bucked, passengers laughed nervously.

The flight attendants had hastily removed the drink carts and were sitting at the back doing crossword puzzles. The woman sitting next to Susan excused herself and rushed toward the bathroom, holding her hand in front of her mouth as she hurried down the fun-house-lurching aisle. When she returned, her companion was staring at his Bible. Having traded seats with Susan, Elijah then said some words to the sick woman that Susan couldn't hear, whereupon the woman nodded and seemed to calm down.

How strange it was, his ability to give comfort. He doled it out in every direction. He wasn't just trained as a doctor; he was a doctor all the way down to the root. Looking over at him, at his hair flecked with early gray, she thought uneasily of his generosity and its possible consequences, and then, in almost the same moment, she felt overcome with pride and love.


In Prague, the Soviet-era hotel where they stayed smelled of onions, chlorine, and goulash. The lobby had mirrored ceilings. Upstairs, the rooms were small and claustrophobic; the TV didn't work, and all the signs were nonsensical. *Pozor!* for example, which seemed to mean "Beware!" Beware of what? The signs were garbles of consonants. Prague wasn't Kafka's birthplace for nothing. Still, Susan believed the city was the perfect place for them to conceive a child. For the first one, you always needed some sexual magic, and this place had a particular old-world variety of it. As for Elijah, he seemed to be in a mood: early on their second morning in the hotel, he stood in front of the window rubbing his scalp and commenting on Prague's air quality. "Stony, like a castle," he said. Because he always slept naked, he stood before the window naked, with a doctor's offhandedness about the body, surveying the neighborhood. She thought he resembled the pope blessing the multitudes in Vatican Square, but no: on second thought he didn't resemble the pope at all, starting with the nakedness. A sexual sentimentalist, he loved the body as much as he loved the spirit: he liked getting down on his knees in front of her nakedness to kiss her belly and incite her to soft moans.

"We should go somewhere," she said, thumbing through a guidebook, which he had already read. "I'd like to see the Old Town Square. We'd have to take the tram there. Are you up for that?"

"Hmm. How about the chapels in the Loreto?" he asked. "That's right up here. We could walk to it in ten minutes and then go to the river." He turned around and approached her, sitting next to her on the bed, taking her hand in his. "It's all so close, we could soak it all up, first thing."

"Sure," she said, although she didn't remember anything from the guidebooks about the Loreto chapels and couldn't guess why he wanted to go see them. He raised her hand to his mouth and kissed her fingers one by one, which always gave her chills.

"Oh, honey," she said, leaning into him. He was the only man she had ever loved, and she was still trying to get used to it. She had done her best not to be scared by the way she often felt about him. His intelligence, the concern for children, the quiet loving homage he paid to her, the wit, the indifference to sports, the generosity, and then the weird secret toughness—where could you find another guy like that? It didn't even matter that they were staying in a bad hotel. Nothing else mattered. "What's in those chapels?" she asked. "How come we're going there?"

"Babies," he told her. "Hundreds of babies." He gave her a smile. "Our baby is in there."

After dressing in street clothes, they walked down Bělohorská toward the spot on the map where the chapel was supposed to be. In the late-summer morning, Susan detected traceries of autumnal chill, a specifically Czech irony in the air, with high wispy cirrus clouds threading the sky like promissory notes. Elijah took her hand, clasping it very hard, checking both ways as they crossed the tramway tracks, the usual *Pozor!* warnings posted on their side of the platform telling them to exercise caution toward ... whatever. The number 18 tram lumbered toward them silently from a distance up the hill to the west.

Fifteen minutes later, standing inside one of the chapels, Susan felt herself soften from all the procreative excess on display. Eli had been right: carved babies took up every available space. Surrounding them on all sides—in the front, at the altar; in the back, near the choir loft, where the carved cherubs played various musical instruments; and on both walls—were plump winged infants in various postures of angelic gladness. She'd never seen so many sculpted babies in one place: cherubs not doing much of anything except engaging in a kind of abstract giggling frolic, freed from both gravity and the Earth, the great play of Being inviting worship. What bliss! God was in the babies. But you had to look up, or you wouldn't see them. The angelic orders were always above you. At the front, the small cross on the altar rested at eye level, apparently trivial, unimportant, outnumbered, in this nursery of angels. For once, the famous agony had been trumped by babies, who didn't care about the Crucifixion or hadn't figured it out.

"They loved their children," Susan whispered to Eli. "They worshipped infants."

"Yeah," Eli said. She glanced up at him. On his face rested an expression of great calm, as if he were in a kingdom of sorts where he knew the location of everything. He *was* a pediatrician, after all. "Little kids were little ambassadors from God in those days. Look at that one." He pointed. "Kind of a lascivious smile. Kind of *knowing*."

She wiped a smudge off his cheek with her finger. "Are you hungry? Do you want lunch yet?"

He dug into his pocket and pulled out a nickel, holding it as if he were about to drop it into her hand. Then he took it back. "We just got here. It's not lunchtime. We got out of bed less than two hours ago. I love you," he said matter-of-factly, apropos of nothing. "Did I already tell you this morning? I love you like crazy." His voice rose with an odd conviction. The other tourists in the chapel glanced at them. Was their love that obvious? Outside, the previous day, sitting near a fountain, Susan had seen a young man and a young woman, lovers, steadfastly facing each other and stroking each other's thighs, both of them crazed with desire and, somehow, calm about it.

"Yes," she said, and a cool wind passed through her at that

moment, right in through her abdomen and then out the back near her spine. "Yes, you do, and thanks for bringing me here, honey, and I agree that we should go to the Kafka Museum, too, but you know what? We need to see if we can get tickets to *The Marriage of Figaro* tonight, and anyway I want to walk around for a while before we go back to that hotel."

He looked down at her. "That's interesting. You didn't say you loved me now." His smile faded. "I said I love you, and you mentioned opera tickets. I hope I'm not being petty, but my love went out to you and was not returned. How come? Did I do something wrong?"

"It was an oversight. No, wait a minute. You're wrong. I did say that. I *did* say I love you. I say it a lot. You just didn't hear me say it this time."

"No, I don't think that's right," he said, shaking his head like a sad horse, back and forth. "You didn't say it."

"Well, I love you *currently*," she said, as a group of German tourists waddled in through the entranceway. "I love you this very minute." She waited. "What a poor excuse for a quarrel this is. Let's talk about something else."

"There," he said, pointing to a baby-angel. "How about that one? That one will be ours. The doctor says so." The angel he had pointed to had wings, as they all did, but this one's arms were outstretched as if in welcome, and the wings were extended as if the angel were about to take flight.

After leaving the chapel, walking down a side street to the old city, they encountered a madwoman with gray snarled hair and only two visible teeth who was carrying a shopping bag full of scrap cloth. She had caught up to them on the sidewalk, emerging from an alleyway, and she began speaking to them in rapid vehement Czech, poking them both on their shoulders to make her unintelligible points. Everything about her was untranslatable, but given the way she was glaring at them, she seemed to be engaged in prophecy of some kind, and Susan intuited that the old woman was telling them both what their future lives together would be like. "You will eventually go back to your bad hotel, you two," she imagined the old woman saying in Czech, "and you will have your wish, and with that good-hearted husband of yours, you will conceive a child, your firstborn, a son, and you will realize that you're pregnant because when you fall asleep on the night of your son's conception, you will dream of a giant raspberry. How do I know all this? Look at me! It's my business to know. I'm out of my mind." Eli gently nudged the woman away from Susan, taking his wife's hand and crossing the street. When Susan broke free from her husband's grip and looked back, she saw the crone shouting. "You're going to be so terribly jealous of your husband *because of the woman in him!*" the old woman screamed in Czech, or so Susan imagined, but somehow that made no sense, and she was still trying to puzzle it out when she turned around and was gently knocked over by a tram that had slowed for the Malostranské stop.

The following commotion—people surrounding her, Elijah asking her nonsensical diagnostic questions—was all a bit of a blur, but only because everyone except for her husband was speaking Czech or heavily accented English, and before she knew it, she was standing up. She looked at the small crowd assembled around her, tourists and citizens, and in an effort to display good health she saluted them. Only after she had done it, and people were staring, did she think that gestures like that might be inappropriate.

"Good God," Elijah said. "Why'd you do that?"

"I felt like it," she told him.

"Are you okay? Where does it hurt?" he asked, touching her professionally. "Here? Or here?"

"It doesn't hurt anywhere," she said. "I just got jostled. I lost my balance. Can't we go have lunch?" The tram driver was speaking to her in Czech, but she was ignoring him. She glanced down at her jeans. "See? I'm not even scuffed up."

"You almost fell under the wheels," he half groaned.

"Really, Eli. Please. I'm fine. I've never been finer. Can't we go now?" Strangers were still muttering to her, and someone was translating. When they calmed down and went back to their business after a few minutes, she felt a great sense of relief. She didn't want anyone to think of her as a victim. She was no one's and nothing's victim ever. Or: maybe she was in shock.

"So here we are," Eli said. "We've already been to a chapel, seen a baby, talked to a crazy person, had an accident, and it's only eleven."

"Well, all right, let's have coffee, if we can't have lunch."

He held her arm as they crossed the street and made their way to a sidewalk café with a green awning and a signboard that seemed to indicate that the café's name had something to do with a sheep. The sun was still shining madly in its touristy way. Ashtrays (theirs was cracked) were placed on all the tables, and a man with a thin wiry white beard and a beret was smoking cigarette after cigarette nearby. He gazed at Susan and Elijah with intense indifference. Susan wanted to say: *Yes, all right, we're stupid American tourists, like the rest of them, but I was just hit by a tram!* The waiter came out and took their order: two espressos.

"You didn't see that thing coming?" Elijah asked, sitting up and looking around. "My God. It missed me by inches."

"I wasn't hit," she said. "I've explained this to you. I was nudged. I was nudged and lost my balance and fell over. The tram was going about two miles an hour. It happens."

"No," he said. "It *doesn't* happen. When has it ever happened?"

"Eli, it just did. I wasn't thinking. That woman, the one we saw, that woman who was shouting at us . . ."

"She was just a crazy old lady. That's all she was. There are crazy old people everywhere. Even here in Europe. Especially here. They go crazy, history encourages it, and they start shouting, but no one listens."

"No. No. She was shouting at *me*. She had singled me out. That's why I wasn't looking or paying attention. And what's really weird is that I could understand her. I mean, she was speaking in Czech or whatever, but I could understand her."

"Susan," he said. The waiter came with their espressos, daintily placing them on either side of the cracked ashtray. "Please. That's delusional. Don't get me wrong—that's not a criticism. I still love you. You're still beautiful. Man, are you beautiful. It just kills me, how beautiful you are. I can hardly look at you."

"I know." She leaned back. "But listen. Okay, sure, I know it's delusional, I get that, but she said I was going to be jealous of you. That part I didn't get." She thought it was better not to mention that they would have a son.

"Jealous? Jealous of me? For what?"

"She didn't . . . *say.*"

"Well, then."

"She said I'd get pregnant."

"Susan, honey."

"And that I'd dream of a giant raspberry on the night of conception."

"Oh, for Christ's sake. A raspberry. Please stop."

"You're being dismissive. I'm serious. When have I ever said or done anything like this before? Well, all right, maybe a few times. But I *can't* stop."

The man sitting next to them lifted up his beret and held it aloft for a moment before putting it back on his head.

"Yeah, that's right. Thank you," Elijah said to the man. He pulled out a bill, one hundred crowns, from his wallet and dropped it on the table. "Susan, we need to get back to the hotel. Okay? Right now. Please?"

"Why? I'm fine. I've never been better."

He gazed at her. He would take her back to the hotel, pretending to want to make love to her, and he *would* make love to her, but the lovemaking would just be a pretext so that he could do a full hands-on medical examination of her, top to bottom. She had seen him pull such stunts before, particularly in moments when the doctor in him, the force of his caretaking, had overpowered him.

———

What she saw in her dream wasn't a raspberry. The crone had gotten that part wrong. What she saw was a tree, a white pine, growing in a forest alongside a river, and the tree swayed as the wind pushed at it, setting up a breathy whistling sound.

They named their son Raphael, which, like Michael, was an angel's name. Eli claimed that he had always liked being an Elijah, so they had looked up angel-names and prophet-names on Google and quickly discarded the ones like Zadkiel and Jerahmeel that were just too strange: exile-on-the-playground names. Susan's mother thought that naming a child after an angel was extreme bad luck, given the name's high visibility, but once the baby took after Susan's side of the family—he kept a stern gaze on objects of his attention, though he laughed easily, as Susan's father did—the in-laws were eventually softened and stopped complaining about his being a Raphael. Anyway, Old Testament names were coming back. You didn't have to be the child of a midwestern farmer to have one. On their block in San Francisco, an Amos was the child of a mixed-race couple; a Sariel belonged to a gay couple; and Gabriel, a bubbly toddler, as curious as a cat, lived next door.

After they brought Raphael home from the hospital, they set up a routine so that if Eli was home and not at the hospital, he would give Raphael his evening feeding. On a Tuesday night, Susan went upstairs and found Elijah holding the bottle of breast milk in his left hand while their son lay cradled in his right arm. They had painted the room a boy's blue, and sometimes she could still smell the paint. Adhesive stars were affixed to the ceiling.

A small twig snapped inside her. Then another twig snapped. She felt them physically. Looking at her husband and son, she couldn't breathe.

"You're holding him wrong," she said.

"I'm holding him the way I always hold him," Eli said. Raphael continued to suck milk from the bottle. "It's not a big mystery. I *know* how to hold babies. It's what I do."

She heard the sound of a bicycle bell outside. The thick bass line on an overamped car radio approached and then receded down the block. She inhaled with great effort.

"He's uncomfortable. You can tell. Look at the way he's curled up."

"Actually, no," Elijah said, moving the baby to his shoulder to burp him. "You can't tell. He's nursing just fine." From his sitting position, he looked up at her. "This is my job."

"There's something I can't stand about this," Susan told him. "Give me a minute. I'm trying to figure it out." She walked into the room and leaned against the changing table. She glanced at the floor, trying to think of how to say to Eli the strange thought that had an imminent, crushing weight, that she had to say aloud or she would die. "I told you you're not holding him right."

"And I told you that I am."

"Eli, I don't want you feeding him." There. She had said it. "I don't want you nursing him. I'm the mother here. You're not."

"What? You're kidding. You don't want me nursing him? Now? Or ever?"

"I don't want you feeding Raphael. Period."

"That's ridiculous. What are you talking about?"

"I can't stand it. I'm not sure why. But I can't."

"Susan, listen to yourself, listen to what you're saying. You don't get to decide something like this—we both do. I'm as much a parent here as you are. All I'm doing is holding a baby bottle with your breast milk in it while Raphael sucks on it, and then—well, *now*—I'm holding him on my shoulder while he burps." He had a slightly clinical, almost diagnostic expression on his face, checking her out.

"Actually, no, I don't think you're paying attention to what I'm saying." She fixed him with a sad look, even though what she felt was positive rage. Inwardly, she was resisting the impulse to snatch their baby out of his arms. With one part of her mind, she saw this impulse as animal truth, if not actually unique to her; but with another part, she thought: *Every mother feels this way, every mother has felt this, it's time to stand up*. She was not going to chalk this one up to postpartum depression or hormonal imbalances or feminine moodiness. She had come upon this truth, and she would not let it go. She felt herself lifting off. "You can't be his mother. You can't do this. I won't let you."

"You're in a moment, Susan," he said. "You'll get over it."

"No, I won't get over it." Raphael burped onto Eli. "I'll never get over it, and you will not fucking tell me that I will."

"Please stop shouting," he said, ostentatiously calm.

"This is not your territory. This is my territory, and you can't have it."

"Are we going to argue about metaphors? Because that's the wrong metaphor."

"We aren't going to argue about anything. Put him down. Put him into the crib."

Eli stood for a few seconds, and then with painfully executed elaboration he lowered Raphael into the crib and pulled the blue blanket that Eli's mother had made for the baby over him. He started up the music box and turned around. Both his hands were tightened into fists.

"I'm going out," he said. "I've got to go out right now."

She closed her eyes, and when she opened them, he was gone.

She went downstairs and turned on the TV. On the screen— she kept the sound muted because she didn't really want to get attached to the story—a man with an eagle tattoo on his forearm aimed a gun at a distant figure of indistinct gender. The man fired, whereupon the distant figure fell. The screen cut to a brightly lit room where male authority figures of some kind were jotting down notes and answering landline telephones while they held cups of coffee. Perhaps, she thought, this was an old movie. One woman, probably a cop, heard something on the phone and reacted with alarm. Then she shouted at the others in the room, and their shocked faces were instantly replaced by a soap commercial showing a cartoon rhinoceros in a bubble bath set upon by a trickster monkey, and this commercial was then replaced by another one, with grinning skydivers falling together in a geometrical pattern advertising an insurance company, and then the local newscaster came on with a tease for the ten o'clock news, followed by a commercial for a multinational petroleum operation apparently dedicated to cleaning up the environment and saving baby seals, and Susan scratched her foot, and she was looking at the no-longer-distant figure (a young woman, as it turned out) on an autopsy table as a medical examiner pointed at a bullet hole in the victim's rib cage area—tantalizingly close to her breasts, which were demurely covered, though the handheld camera seemed eager to see them—and Susan felt her eyes getting heavy, and then another, older, woman was hit by a tram in Prague, which was how she knew she was dreaming. Sleeping, she wondered when Eli would return. She wondered, for a moment, where her husband had gone.

When she woke up, Eli stood before her, bleeding from the side of his mouth, a bruise starting to form just under his left eye. His knuckles were caked and bloody. On his face was an expression of joyful defiance. He was blocking the TV set. It was as if he had come out of it somehow.

She stood up and reached toward him. "You're bleeding."

He brushed her hand away. "Let me bleed."

"What did you say?"

"You heard me. Let me bleed." He was smilingly jubilant. The smile looked like one of the smiles on the faces of the angels in the Loreto chapel.

"What happened to you?" she asked. "You got into a fight.

My God. We need to put some ice or something on that." She tried to reach for him again, and again he moved away from her.

"Leave me alone. Listen," he said, straightening up, "you want to know what happened? This is what happened. I was angry at you, and I started walking, and I ended up in Alta Plaza Park. I walked in there, you know, where it was dark? Off those steep stairs on Clay Street? And this is the thing. I wanted to kill somebody. That's kind of a new emotion for me, wanting to kill somebody. I mean, I wasn't looking for someone to kill, but that's what I was *thinking*. I'm just trying to be honest here. So I went up the stairs and found myself at the top, with the view, with the famous view of the city. Everybody admires the view, and I looked off into the darkness and thought I heard a scream, somewhere off there in the distance, and so, you know, I went toward it, toward the scream, the way anybody would. So I made my way off into the shadows, and what I saw was this other thing."

"This thing?"

"Yeah, that's right. This other thing. These two guys were beating up this girl, tearing her clothes, and then they had her down, one of them was holding her down, and the other one was, you know, lowering his jeans. No one else was around. So I went in. I wasn't even thinking. I went in and grabbed the guy who was holding her down, and I slugged him. The other one, he got up and punched me in the kidneys. The woman, I think *she* stood up. No, I *know* she stood up because she said something in Spanish, and she ran away. I was fighting these guys, and she took off. She didn't stay. I know she ran because when I hit the guy who was behind me with my elbow, I saw her running away, and I saw that she was barefoot."

"This was in Alta Plaza Park?"

"Yeah."

"That's in Pacific Heights. They don't usually have crime over there."

"Well, they did tonight. I was fighting with those guys, and I finally landed a good one, on the first guy, and I broke his jaw. *I heard it break.* That was when they took off. The second guy took off and the one with the broken jaw was groaning and went after him. No honor among thieves." He smiled. "Goddamn, I feel great."

She lifted his hand and touched the knuckles where scabs were forming. "So you were brave."

"Yes, I was."

"You saved her."

"Anybody would have done it."

"No," she said. "I don't think so."

She led him upstairs and sat him down on the edge of the bathtub. With a washcloth, she dabbed off the blood from his hands and face. There was something about his story she didn't believe, and then for a moment she didn't believe a word of it, but she continued to wash him tenderly as if he were the hero he said he was. He groaned quietly when she touched some newly bruised part of him. He would look terrible for a while. How happy that would make him! She could easily get some steak, or hamburger, or whatever you were supposed to apply to black eyes to make the swelling go away, but no, he wouldn't want that. He would want his badge. They all wanted that.

"Should we go to bed, Doctor?" she asked.

"Yes."

"I love you," she said. They would postpone the argument about feedings until tomorrow, or next week.

"I love you, too."

She undressed him, just as if he were a child, before lowering him onto the sheets. He sighed loudly. She could hear Raphael's breaths coming from the nursery. She was about to go into her son's room to check on him and then thought better of it. Standing in the hallway, she heard a voice asking, "What will you do with another day?" Who had asked that? Eli was asleep. Anyway, it was a nonsensical question. The air had asked it, or she was hearing voices. She went into the bathroom to brush her teeth. She didn't quite recognize her own face in the mirror, but the reflected swollen tender breasts were still hers, and the smile, when she thought of sweet Elijah bravely fighting someone, somewhere—that was hers, too.

# *Loyalty*

As much as I love her, I blame Astrid. Astrid told my wife, Corinne, that she could achieve happiness if only she'd leave me. It sounded simple. "Leave that guy, walk out that door, you'll achieve happiness, you'll be free." Achieve happiness. Now there's a phrase. Into the Ford with the busted shocks and out onto the American road, then—that was the prescription.

I stood in the driveway. It was sleeting the day she left. I had agreed not to follow her. She was so eager to go, she forgot to use the windshield wipers until she was halfway down the block. She turned the corner, the tires splashed slush, the front end dipped from the bad shocks, and she was gone.

Holding on to my son, I walked into the garage, taking an inventory. Jeremy, in my arms. My rusting pickup truck. The broken rake, the bent saw, the corroded timing light still on the ledge beneath the back window with the curtains. Yes, the garage window had curtains. Don't ask me why I put them there. More inventory: the house itself. My life. My health. My job. A case of beer. My mother, Dolores, upstairs in her room. *Let them arrive here,* whatever they are, is my first motto, and my second is *Let them stay.*

Astrid thought that happiness was within poor Corinne's grasp, and she said so, day after day. Happiness for you, she would say, is a day without Wes. You are right to say that Wes crowds you and confuses you. Any morning you wake up without that guy's stale beer breath on you will be pure profit. Astrid was relentless on the subject of me. She and Corinne worked at the same nurses' station, 3-F. In the quiet of the hospital night, plans were hatched. A nurse can always get a job, anyplace. Those were Astrid's words, I have no doubt.

Corinne had been bitching about me, to me, and the topics were, I don't know, the usual. I drank too much on weekends, my dog, Scooter, slobbered on the bedroom floor, my hands were always dirty from the shop—and the killer accusation: I was inattentive to her needs, whatever they were. Mostly Corinne complained about herself, her rickety soiled unrecognizable life, her confusion, her panic over our baby, her fear of being an inadequate mother, her sadness, that stuff.

But I loved her, and she left me. Then I loved Astrid, and I married her. I'm married to her now, and I still love her. She has—and I've got to use this word—guile. Corinne, my first wife, had none. You'd think a nurse of all people could take care of her own baby and not be bewildered. But she was. Mousy brown hair, mystified by most conversations, unable to fix a dinner you could serve to guests, she was about the most lovable thing you ever saw. I lost my heart to her helplessness time and again. I'm not saying this is admirable.

The minute Corinne was gone, Astrid showed up. I don't recall that, prior to that day, we had so much as exchanged a moody, sparking glance. She took me into her expert arms. It was consolation and sympathy at first, I guess. I didn't question it. In about the time it takes to change the painted background in a photographer's studio from a woodland scene to a brick wall, she had left her boyfriend and was presenting me with casseroles and opened bottles of cold beer. I took some advantage of her, but she didn't mind my advances. She was saying, "Wes, it seems you are the one. I am surprised." She discounted the flaws I owned up to. My first wife lost her credibility as a character witness, and I got a spell cast on me. And then I softened. Love for Astrid like a climbing vine grew out of my heart. I don't know how else to say it.

She was competent and assured with child rearing, calm in the face of infant tantrums. On Sunday morning, next to me, Astrid would read the travel section, pencil in hand, naming far-flung places we would go someday. In this household, confusion was dispelled. Now we had pedestals. Things like clarity and plans and pleasure and love went on top of them. What luck I'd been given, I thought. Here was all this day-in-day-out whoopee. Astrid brought all surfaces to an unlikely shine. Jeremy stopped yelling all the time and began to grow. Teeth, toddling, jabber, talk.

New toys appeared. The divorce went through without Corinne wanting any custody whatsoever or getting any. Astrid and I married, and pretty soon we had ourselves another child, a startlingly beautiful daughter. Lucy. A new path, the next stage.

Corinne called Jeremy when he was grown enough to talk, but she couldn't manage to see him, or so she said in her jumbled, haphazard way. She was too delicate, and she claimed her strings were too tightly strung for ordinary social life. Visits would put stress on her immune system. Anyway, she couldn't manage them, or so she said. Jeremy suffered from this absence, but when it became permanent, he didn't suffer anymore because Astrid had taken over the mom chores with such competence and love. So Corinne called instead of visiting, and mostly she wrote letters.

My God, those letters! Moms aren't supposed to write letters like that. The coffee spills, the anarchic handwriting, the paragraphs without topics, the sentences without subjects and verbs. Jeremy's letters back to Corinne were full of the news of his childhood. After a while, his letters became very halfhearted, quoting baseball statistics. He wrote them with decreasing frequency.

The time when Corinne went on daytime TV, the show was about runaway moms. She sat on the stage with three other women. What made her willing to appear there, I'll never know. For the first ten minutes, the foppish host of the show and the question-askers from the audience sounded reasonable and sympathetic, but by the end of the hour, they were indignant. Out in the peanut gallery they were pointing fingers and shouting at the runaway moms, and others applauded and woofed when the accusations concluded. I only heard about it from a neighbor who watches TV all day and who said that Corinne's hair was darker than she remembered it, with gray streaks.

I felt terrible for Corinne, for her eager incompetence and wish to be on national television. I could imagine her befuddled face as she sat there being razzed by hooligans in the studio.

Dolores, my mother, came to live with us in the spare room upstairs right before Corinne left. She said she'd help with Jeremy, and she did for a while. Mostly she stayed up there knitting and staring out the window, checking for strangers to our neighborhood, including door-to-door salesmen. On Thursdays she would go to her bridge club and on Friday nights to Bible study. Despite her name (*dolores* means "sad" according to the Latin), my mother is quite upbeat. *Take a chance on life* is her motto. She and Astrid bonded immediately. She has tried to keep it a secret from me, but I know my mother was and is interested in extraterrestrials (although she is a registered Republican) and believes that Jesus will be back any day now. She imagines that we are in the end-time and must meet the challenges of life with Christian dignity.

Astrid humors her, though they avoid this topic when I am in the room.

My mother's help was not required after our daughter, Lucy, was born. But Lucy was never any trouble at all. She could have raised herself. She came out of the birth canal with an accusing look on her face directed at me.

Jeremy is seventeen and has a tattoo of a Japanese word on his left calf. I still don't know what it means, and he won't say. On his hip is another tiny tattoo, a grinning gremlin, hands on hips. It's illegal for children and adolescents to get tattoos, but he evidently got them in a low place known only to his set. I read Jeremy the riot act that time he came home with the Japanese character but was treated with amused, affectionate scorn, as if I were a historical artifact. Get this: in deep winter he's been known to wear a sweatshirt, jeans, and flip-flops outside. Summer clothes in a snowstorm— a pretense of immortality. He wants to be a young god as they all do and defy the seasons. In Minnesota that's a brave stand, and many teenage boys take it. Therefore he's wildly popular. He has several hundred friends and is constantly texting them. His face has some of the sweet beauty of his mother, Corinne. The three women in the household dote on him. They comb his hair and would tie his shoelaces for him if he'd let them. His little sister sketches his face when he is sitting down. Imagine the possible result: a spoiled brat. However, he's not really spoiled, just blasé. Naturally he smiles all the time, having done nothing to earn all this love. He looks past me as if I were a footnote.

The point is, Corinne is back in town, and we have a situation on our hands. She has sent a postcard saying that she will be arriving by bus, and so I take a few hours off from work at the garage to go downtown to get her. Explanations for her arrival? None. Some idea of what the agenda might be? Not a clue. Her arrival has no more rationale than her departure did all those years ago.

Although I am not secretive by nature, I have told no one else in the house about Corinne's reappearance. When I arrive at the Greyhound station on Hawthorne Avenue, I enter the doors and smell that rich bus-station smell of humus mixed with nitrates. You feel like editorializing on humanity when you enter a bus station. But you don't, because Corinne is already sitting there, waiting on a bench. She has two brown paper bags with her. Soiled clothes are peeking out of the tops of the bags, sweaters and unmentionables, and she's staring at the wall clock.

And here I must try to describe my ex-wife in her current condition.

Imagine a beautiful woman of middle age who has somehow gone through a car wash. She has dried out, but the car wash has rumpled her up, left the hair going every which way, and on her face is a dazed expression and she has new parallel lines on her forehead and crow's-feet around her eyes. Life has worried and picked at her. But that's not the point. The point is that she's still beautiful to me, which is strange. It's counter to common sense.

She's wearing a pink sweatshirt with the name of a TV show printed on it. It's the TV show she was on and where she was mocked. The show's name is the name of the small-minded and mean millionaire host with the thin mustache. Corinne looks up at me as I take her hand. She stands audibly. She kisses me on the cheek. For that instant her warm lips are familiar. I feel an antiquated tingle.

"Wes," she says, "I knew you'd save me."

"Haven't saved you yet, Corinne," I say, trying to laugh it off. She smells of french fries and hamburger and ketchup. A fast-food smell. The poor soul. What's happened to her? "How are you?"

"How am I? As you can see."

I don't say anything in the face of the incomparable wreckage she presents.

"Well," she says, "is the inspection over? Would you take one of these bags? I'll take the other." She picks up one of the aforementioned bags, and when I look down I see that her shoes are split at the seams. Through the hole in her left shoe, toes are visible.

My first wife has become a bag lady, and here she is.

———

This is what she says in the truck on the way back to the house.

"It's the economy. There's suffering. You were always a grease monkey, Wes, and you could always get a job fixing cars. So you wouldn't know. But they're making it really personal in my case and saying that I can't keep track of things. Perhaps I *was* losing track, but only in the afternoons when I was off by myself, and the experts wouldn't deny that, although they tried to. In a way, the multinational banks did this to me, because I couldn't live on my income and I was eventually fired from the hospital, and even though sorrow isn't necessarily contagious, I know I caught it directly from one of my patients. He was a man who groaned all day. The groans got into my head and took up residence there. I'm hearing them now. Can you hear them? No? Lucky you. God bless you for picking me up, Wes. I know I should have given you more of a warning, but I couldn't. My goodness, it's cold." She wraps a scarf around her neck. But it's not cold. The cold is all in her head. It's a warm and humid early October day, seventy degrees. Indian summer. To stay warm and to give herself a greenhouse effect, she's wrapped herself up like a mummy.

"That's all right, Corinne," I tell her. "Where are you staying, by the way?"

She looks at me.

"What I meant was, how long are you staying? Here? With us?"

Gazing out, she says, "American cities are so dirty." She points to an abandoned, boarded-up drugstore. "I do remember an apothecary, and hereabouts a-dwells," she says meaninglessly, as if she's quoting from somewhere. She breathes in deeply and coughs twice. "Let me tell you a story. There was this woman. And she was just fine for a while, and her husband was just fine, too, and no one was to blame for anything. Let's say this happened in the past. They lived in comfort and kindness with each other. But then something happened. Let's say a volcano erupted. And she never knew what happened, I mean who caused the volcano, but she knew something did happen, because gradually she was never fine. The dust made her cough, and the water seemed to be poisoned, and the air smelled terrible, of lava, and there were voices, and she realized she had made a big mistake bringing a child into the world. Into this world, my God, how terrible it is, and no one has any idea."

"Oh, Corinne," is all I can say. Trouble is waiting for me patiently at home. Because I have not told Astrid, my wife, or Dolores, my mother, or Jeremy, my son, or Lucy, my daughter, that Corinne is in town, there will be tribulation. Why couldn't I tell anyone that I was going to the bus station to pick her up? I know why. Give me some credit. After all these years, I wanted to see her, and therefore I would see her. I had forgiven her. I forgive her now. But would they? It was a bad bet. Still, I am the head of the household.

She pulls down the sun visor and moves the little slide to the left and looks at herself in the visor's mirror, primping her hair. "They've done things to me. They don't let up."

"I know."

"Wes," she says, turning to face me, "I can't help it. I need taking care of for a time."

The neutrality on her face has vanished. There is another

expression there now. It is one of supplication such as you see from homeless veterans on street corners. *Supplication.* Does anybody ever use that word in normal life? I doubt it.

"There's something I want you to do," she says, but then she won't say what it is. "Is this your neighborhood?" she asks.

"We're getting there," I say.

Houses pass by, old houses with large front porches, and I note a screech from my F-150's engine, a loose fan belt.

"Wes, did you ever think of me?"

It's a trick question. They are always asking you for outright expressions of affection and love. But I have to be careful. My answer may be quoted back to me. For a moment I am spooked.

"Yes, I did think of you. Often."

"Even after you were married to Astrid?"

"Yes." I drive down a full city block before I say, "I worried about you."

This is not the answer she has been fishing for. But she seems to relax and to settle back. On the floor of the truck, on the passenger side, there is an empty beer can I forgot to throw out. With a regal air, she puts her right foot on it to keep it from rolling around.

"I thought that maybe you did. Sometimes I had dreams about you. In the dreams you were a young man, and you were still being kind to me. You carried me once out of a burning apartment house. You did it for free. In the dream."

---

We pull into the driveway. I can see from the blue Honda Civic parked in the garage that Astrid is already home. My mother—today is Wednesday—will certainly be upstairs in her room knitting a shawl or surfing the Internet for stories about true crime or the coming apocalypse. Jeremy may still be out tomcatting around town with his crazed friends before dinner, but Lucy will be in residence in the living room, reading one of her horse books.

Really, I should take Corinne to a motel until I can figure out what to do with her. But instead I pick up her two brown paper bags. We go in through the side door, stop for a moment in the mudroom, and then go up the three stairs into the kitchen past several pairs of soiled empty shoes. I'm behind her, and I notice how gray her hair has become and how it, too, gives off a fast-food odor.

In the kitchen, Astrid has been sprinkling seasoning onto some salmon when she glances up and sees Corinne, who looks worse than she did a few minutes ago because of the kitchen's overhead light. First Astrid looks at Corinne. Then she looks at me, and then she looks at Corinne again. Expressions pass across her face so quickly that you might think you hadn't seen the previous one before the next one appears. First she's confused: her eyebrows rise up. Who's that? Then she's in full recognition mode: her mouth opens, slightly, though she says nothing. Her tongue licks her upper lip. Then it's time for pity and compassion, and her eyes start to water. Then she's shocked, and her hand with lemon juice on it rises to her face. "Uh," she says, but nothing else comes out. A little spot of seasoning stays on her cheek. Then she's angry, and that's when she looks at me, as if I were the cause of all this. But the anger doesn't stay posted up there on her face for long. It's displaced by an expression we don't have a word for. You see this expression when someone is hit by circumstances that are much bigger than expected, and the person is trying to restore things to normal, which can't be done. Actors can't duplicate this look. It only happens in real life.

My wife makes a move toward my ex-wife, to embrace her. I stand there waiting to see whether there will be an implausible hug. But Astrid stops herself in midstep.

Right about then, Lucy sails into the kitchen, heading toward the refrigerator for a diet soft drink. She turns and sees Corinne. "Who're you?" she asks rudely.

No one remembers to say anything in response. Down the street, in the distance, a car alarm goes off, a faint *eee eee eee* sound.

Lucy looks at me, then at her mother, then at Corinne. "What's going on?"

"This," I say at last, pointing at Corinne, "is Jeremy's mother, Corinne. She's here for a visit."

"How do you do?" Corinne says. "You must be Lucy. You look so clean. And bright. So do you, Astrid," she says, smiling at my wife. "But then you always did. It must be from the hospital. It must be from the disinfectants."

"My God, Corinne," Astrid blurts out. "What happened to you?"

"I died," Corinne says. "And then I got on a bus and came here."

———

Astrid tells me that she and I need to talk, and we descend into the mudroom to confer. I explain about the postcard, and Astrid nods randomly. She's angry, of course, that I said that Corinne was, or is, Jeremy's mother. She's even angrier that she's here and that I had said nothing about her arrival, but given the strangeness of events, I am temporarily forgiven. We determine that for now Corinne will sleep in the basement rec room's foldout bed. She may find the basement somewhat damp, given her allergic inclinations, but that's life. The dehumidifier does its level best. Then Astrid says to me, "Don't ever do this again," as if Corinne's appearance here is my idea.

"I didn't do it *this* time," I reply.

When we return to the kitchen, my mother has descended from her upstairs room and is talking to Corinne as if Corinne had only been away for a few days. My mother is immune to surprise. Those two are conversing quite lucidly on various topics: the weather, and then recipes they once shared, and treatments for the common cold (zinc lozenges). Astrid returns to the salmon. Will there be enough for everyone? Yes, if the portions are small. I instruct Lucy to set the table, which she does, happy to have a task to keep her occupied. I remind her to set an extra place for Corinne. I pick up Corinne's two brown paper bags and take them downstairs, and I fold out the bed and make it up with sheets and blankets that we keep down there in an old dresser near the dehumidifier.

But what I am thinking about is Jeremy, and so I go back upstairs, past the kitchen, into the living room, and then out into the front yard, and I open my cell phone, and I call him, and when he answers, I say, "Get right home."

He says, "I'm almost there. What's up?"

"Something has happened," is all I can say, "and it's about you. I'll explain when you get home."

Most people don't realize that in an automobile repair shop, you see a wide variety of human behavior in reaction to bad news. Some people practice stoicism. But most of the time, if you tell someone that his car's transmission is shot and will require thousands of dollars of work, you see anger directed *against the automobile*. Or against fate. Or against God for having had a hand in bum transmissions. Or against me, for serving as messenger. The anger is pointless. Life does us no favors. We have to manage with what we have. I'm not complaining. I've had a good life so far. I played tackle in high school football and chased girls and always loved cars. I raised some hell, mostly petty vandalism and a bit of promiscuity and public drunkenness, before I settled down with Corinne. I did my share of drugs. So what? I was crazy the way young men often are. I'm proud to say I was never hauled in before the authorities when I got really wild. My friends watched out for me, and I therefore survived my youth. Because of that, I give thanks for my health and my family. I got my associate's degree. Like I say, I've got no complaints.

But Corinne broke my heart when she left me, and I was ready to be angry with her for years after that. That's a long time ago. Day by day the anger seeped out of me in a slow trickle until it was gone. I have to let her remain here if she wants to. She's wreckage. It's as simple as that. We have these obligations to our human ruins. What happened to her could've happened to me or to anybody.

Jeremy, however, possesses neither wisdom nor adult perspective, and my heart is thumping away like a maddened rabbit in a cage as I wait for him to get home. At last I see him coming down the block on his skateboard while he talks on his cell phone.

When I get to the kitchen, he's standing there near the stove, and all the women are looking at him but no one is saying anything. Again, the silence. What's the matter with them? They talk all the time when nothing is on the line, but if something serious happens, they clam up.

"What's going on?" he asks. He looks over at Corinne and nods his head in her direction. "Who's this?" Corinne is standing over there, propped up against the refrigerator.

Again a silence persists. No one will step up to the plate. So I say, "This is Corinne. Corinne, this is Jeremy."

The thing is, they look so similar that you'd never mistake them for anything except a mother and her son. Gazing at Corinne, Jeremy suddenly notices that resemblance, and he flinches.

"Hi," Corinne says shyly. She sweeps the bangs away from her forehead and gives him a halfhearted smile. She can't hug him. She can't kiss him. Not yet. All she can do is stand there.

Jeremy looks at her, then at Astrid, then at Dolores, and finally at Lucy. That's when Lucy pipes up. "That's your mom," she says as if this were the Ripley's Believe It or Not! museum.

Jeremy points at Astrid. "*That's* my mom."

"Well, we both are, sort of," Corinne says. "Don't you think?" She looks like a high school girl at a dance hoping that some eligible fellow will come into view to retrieve her.

"You're kidding," Jeremy says.

"Corinne is going to stay with us for a while until she gets back on her feet," I say.

That's when he turns to me, blushing from anger. "On her feet?" He starts to leave the room, but then Corinne points at his ear.

"You have an earring," she says. Jeremy nods, stumped by the obvious. And then she says, "I've never gotten used to them on men. Not even on grown men. I know I should, the way everyone else does, but I can't. I just can't." She seems to be trying to break up the silences with plain speech. "No one told me how boy-pretty you'd become. I'm so old-fashioned. With that earring you look a little queer."

"Corinne!" my mother says, leaning against the kitchen counter for stability. "You can't say that. No one says that."

"Yes," she says shamefacedly. "No one does say anything like what I say. It's been my downfall."

"It's all right," Jeremy says. "Because I am queer. I'm, like, a *total* fag. And now this queer is going upstairs. Goodbye."

Off he goes, clumping noisily away from us. I'll let him sit up there for a minute before I go up to talk to him.

"Anyhow," Lucy says, "the word is 'gay.' You can't say 'queer' unless you are queer."

"They're the same, aren't they? Those words?" Corinne asks, trying to smile. I truly wish she would stop talking.

"Well, what's really interesting," Astrid says, suddenly

turning around and facing us, "is why Jeremy would say that he's gay when all the evidence is to the contrary. And there's been quite a bit of evidence already, Corinne, though you wouldn't know that."

"No, I wouldn't know," Corinne responds.

"Tell her about Alissa," Lucy says to her mother. "Little Miss Princess? The pink stockings? The locket? The bunny factory?"

"No, we're not going into that," Astrid says.

"At least he didn't get her pregnant," I say helpfully, because he didn't. They used condoms.

"But he could of," Lucy says proudly. "If he had tried."

"This is *so* the wrong topic," Astrid says. "Corinne, you must be very tired. We're all surprised to see you, as no doubt you know, and I suppose you'd like a glass of water. Are you hungry? Thirsty? The salmon will be ready soon, and we'll all sit down to eat. I wish you had given us a bit of notice. And we'll have to catch up on all your news!" Astrid tries a smile.

"I don't have any news," Corinne says. "Well, I mean, it's all news, it's all news to me. What *isn't* news? This bright shiny kitchen is news! And Lucy: you certainly are the newest thing." She looks at all of us, one by one. "Oh, have pity on me," she says, and then she begins to cry, and all the women move toward her.

Once I'm upstairs, I knock on Jeremy's door. He doesn't say "Come in," but I go in anyway. I'll spare you the details of his room. He's lying on his bed with his eyes closed. His shoes are off and his big feet are sticking up at the end of the bed in their white socks, and he has an arm flung across his face, covering his eyes. I am amazingly proud of my son. I love him so much, but I have to hide it.

"Jeremy," I say. "You'll have to come back down eventually."

"I can't."

"Why not?"

"Because it's unfair. She's unfair. I mean, she's, like, crazy. And I . . . and I'm supposed to love her, or something? Because she was once my mother? Fuck that."

"I need to say something to you," I say. "I just can't think of what."

"Please, Dad. None of that wisdom shit, okay? I hate wisdom. I just fucking hate it."

"Okay," I say. "You're in luck. I don't have any."

"That's good. Can we talk about something else? No, I know: let's *not* talk."

So we don't talk for a minute or two. Then Jeremy says, "You know, this isn't so bad."

"What?"

"Oh, having your mother show up and act crazy. That's not so bad. I mean, you know how I'm studying world geography now?"

"Uh-huh."

"And, like, the point of world geography is not where the countries *are*, but what people actually *do*, you know? I mean, take a country like, for example, Paraguay. You know where Paraguay is, right?"

I nod. But I actually don't know where it is. Near Bolivia?

"So"—and here he sits up—"so, okay. Anyhow, Paraguay is like this nothing country in the middle of South America, and they don't even all speak Spanish there, but this weird Indian language like Sioux except it's South American, but the point is, when you look at conditions, it's not all happy days down there. Well, maybe it's happier now. But what our textbook said? Was that they had, you know, torture parties there. Once. Where torturers get drunk and turn the dial up to eleven. Like they did in Chile. And Argentina. People get their fingernails pulled out and electrodes and stuff. I read about it. I've been reading about it. Torture. Like in Cuba, and in Europe when it was medieval? And in Russia. They'd hook you up to an electric board and zap you. And your body would dance around on the electric table. *Total* pain. I mean, compared to torture, this is nothing." He lies back on his pillow. He closes his eyes. "My mother showing up and being crazy? That is nothing. That's not even waterboarding."

He gives me this lecture while staring at me with great bravery.

I go back downstairs, and the five of us have dinner. Jeremy doesn't join us. That night, lying in bed and looking up at the ceiling fan in the dark of our bedroom, Astrid and I agree that I will have to investigate halfway houses for Corinne, and I will have to get her to a shrink so her moods can be stabilized.

The next morning, Jeremy does not join us for breakfast, and when I look outside, his bicycle is gone. And then, somewhat to my surprise, Corinne reappears in the morning light uncomplaining, saying that she experienced a good sleep. What will my ex-wife do all day? My mother says that she will look after Corinne for now. Perhaps they will go for walks, and my mother will expound about Jesus and how He is coming again to gather us up. As for Jeremy, he can't be upset forever. Lucy gives me a goodbye-daddy kiss before she boards the school bus. She seems unaffected by recent events, but then Corinne is not her mother, and she probably wants life to get back to normal.

That afternoon around four o'clock, as I am writing up a repair order on a faulty water pump, Jeremy comes bicycling into the garage. He looks around and sniffs appreciatively. He surveys the containers of brake fluid shelved in the Parts Department. I don't want him to give me any shit in here in front of my coworkers, so I don't smile although I am glad to see him.

"Hey," I say.

"Hey," he replies. He takes off his helmet and shakes out his hair. He's impressive: you can see why girls love him.

I put down my ballpoint pen. We walk into the customers' lounge and sit down on two vinyl chairs in the corner, next to a table on which are scattered old issues of *Field & Stream* and *Cosmopolitan*. All the customers are gone, so we're there alone. Jeremy stares at me for a moment, as if it's my fault that I met Corinne in the first place and made love to her eighteen years ago, so that he was born.

"Dad, I'm fucked up," he says. "And it's really fucked up that she's here. I'm just saying."

"I know," I reply. "It's hard on all of us."

"Not as hard on you as it is on me. I didn't think I could go back home today."

"Where else could you go?"

"Somewhere," he says. "Friends." It's true: he has many friends he could stay with. "I could actually, like, move out." He waits. "But I'm not going to."

"What are you going to do?" I ask. I have neither wisdom nor advice for him. All I have is curiosity.

"So I went to school this morning? And I found Alissa. I mean, we're over, but we're still friends, sort of. And I'm like, 'My birth mom showed up, and she's fucking nuts, and also she said I looked gay,' and Alissa is like, 'Yeah, wow, but she's your mom and thinks you're cute and you're way *not* gay,' and I go, 'Who gives a shit?' and she's, 'You should,' and I say, 'But she's crazy,' and this is when Alissa sort of gets that lightbulb look and says, 'Well, the cool thing would be to put it all on your Tumblr. That'd be so great. 'Cause if your birth mom's so weird and interesting, everybody will want to read it. Like: "Guess what, everybody, my mom showed up."'"

Somehow I have the feeling this has become a huge business with his friends within the past few hours and that they all have opinions about what he should do.

"And?" I ask.

"That's what's weird," he says. "Like half of my friends already want to know if she's got a blog herself. Because they want to check it out, like right now."

"Maybe you could help her with a blog," I say, trying to mediate. "Maybe you could help her set one up."

"Yeah, I guess I can do that. But I have to hate her for a

few more days." He sits there quietly. "I have to really hate her a few days. I know she's crazy. I *get* that. But I have to hate her for not being loyal to us." He used that word: *us.* As much as I love Astrid, she didn't use that word last night. It was all *you:* you have to do this or that.

So I tell Jeremy that he can hate Corinne for a while, and then he has to give it up.

The hatred lasts longer than we think it will. In the meantime we get Corinne to a psychiatrist, who puts her on lithium. There are no discernible effects at first.

Corinne tries to be inconspicuous down there in the basement and at dinnertime. I'll give her credit for that. It's hard for her, however, because right out of the blue at dinner she'll start talking about wildlife creatures, some of them imaginary, that no one has mentioned in conversation. Wolves and lemurs figure prominently in her thinking, and all the while Jeremy is seething over there at his place at the table. He stares at Corinne with distaste as he bolts his food before he rushes upstairs and slams his bedroom door.

Three weeks later the atmosphere in the house begins to shift subtly, as if a low-pressure system had arrived after a long period of drought. One evening I am coming up the stairs and I see Jeremy and Corinne talking on the landing. Then, two days later, I see her in his room, sitting at his desk in front of his computer, and Jeremy is standing behind her, quietly giving her advice. I know better than to ask them what's going on, so I knock on Lucy's door and go in there. Lucy hears everything that's going on in the house before anyone else does. It's true that she likes to preach, but she has the soul of a Soviet spy.

"Hi, Princess," I say. She's lying on the bed reading a Harry Potter book.

"Hi," she says.

"You okay?" I ask.

"Um, yeah." She has her head propped up by an arm under her chin. On her wall she has a poster of some ballet star up on her toes surrounded by other pink-tutu-clad ladies. Adhesive stars decorate Lucy's ceiling, and her lifelong doll, Eleanor, gazes at her with glassy plastic eyes from the bookshelf. Lucy continues to read while she talks to me.

"What's going on between Corinne and Jeremy? Do you know?"

"You should ask them."

"I can't," I say.

"So," she says, putting the huge novel aside and looking up at me, "he's helping her with *Runaway Mom*." She waits for my reaction, and when I don't say anything, she says, "He got tired of hating her. He decided she wasn't going to go away."

"What's *Runaway Mom*?"

"That's her blog," Lucy says, sitting up and stretching. "He's helping her with it. It's going to be real popular. All the kids at school want to read it."

"What? Why?"

"Daddy, didn't you ever want to run away?"

"No," I say. "I don't think I ever did."

"That's weird," she says. "Everyone else does."

———

Corinne lives across town now, in a little one-bedroom apartment. My mother goes over there on Friday and takes her to Bible class. Corinne gets disability payments from the government, although we worry that those funds will soon be cut off. She comes over here once or twice a week for lunch or dinner. Everyone is mostly getting used to her and her ways, but Astrid has taken up smoking cigarettes (though not my brand) on the front lawn after dinner, a bold move for a woman in midlife.

One time I went to Corinne's blog. Just one time. I opened up *Runaway Mom,* and I read what Corinne had written there a day or two before.

*How many chapters does life have? It has many chapters, and you'll notice that when the passenger train you're on is headed in the wrong direction, it's often moving so fast that you can't get off it without hurting yourself. I threw myself off the particular train I was on and was seriously injured for years. I wish I knew what God wanted from us. I don't think He wants anything from me anymore, but I think He once did, and He said so. Sometimes you run away to leave something behind, and sometimes you run away to get somewhere. I did both. At least I didn't kill myself. At least I didn't murder anyone.*

That was all I wanted to read of her blog. I went out to the garage and opened a beer and smoked a few cigarettes out there in silence. I was thinking.

When I was about eight years old, I took my sled out to one of the city parks. This was the day after a huge snowfall, many inches, but the sledding hill was packed down by the time I got there, and quite a few kids had their boards and saucers and sleds, and they were all screaming happily. I climbed up that hill and flew down on my sled, and after about thirty minutes I was screaming happily, too. I was out there so long I got frostbite on the tips of my toes, and when I came home my mother put me into the bathtub with luke-warm water. I was so happy, I didn't care about the frostbite, and it didn't hurt too much. It just burned. And I didn't think I would remember that day—you don't really think you're going to remember those times when you're happy—but I did. It's funny, the staying power of happiness. I finish my cigarette and put out the stub in the empty beer can.

I can hear Astrid calling to me out the back door. "Wes?" she says. "Wes? Where are you?"

"Out here," I yell from the garage.

"Come in, honey," she calls to me. "It's suppertime."

So I get up from the floor and go into the house, where they are all waiting for me.

# Chastity

On a Wednesday morning while he'd been shaving, Benny Takemitsu heard a woman's scream from down the block. He'd propped open the bedroom window with an old hardback that he planned to read someday, and the May air, carrying the scream, blew in softly over his desk and made the papers tremble. He rushed to the window, the soap still on his throat. How far away was this woman? Benny couldn't tell. And what kind of danger was she in? Nothing was specified. The scream began on one tone and then rose higher as it increased in intensity like a police siren.

Through the venetian blinds, he saw the early-morning sunlight flooding everything, including the blossoming lilacs near his building. Two floors below, a jogger accompanied by a border collie had stopped, and both the jogger and the dog were turned in the same direction.

Benny felt the scream burrowing into his body. The sudden jolt of adrenaline made his heart race and his hands clench. Maybe the screaming woman was in an apartment somewhere, screaming at her husband; maybe he'd forgotten her birthday.

After he finished shaving, Benny sat down on the chair and put on his socks, thinking of the miscellaneous human noises that had disturbed him after he had moved into this building. Two blocks down, a corner bar, Schnitzler's, became a pandemonium factory during summer nights. At closing time, young men, emptied out onto the sidewalk, would bellow their warrior-challenges into the darkness, and the women occasionally lifted their voices in high-pitched alcoholic outcries. Lying in bed, Benny imagined their flushed, belligerent, happy faces.

And the young couple in the next apartment over! During the summer, when their windows were open, their prideful love-yelps acquired carrying power. One of these days, she'd get pregnant, and then her baby would do all the screaming.

At his desk, he moved aside some bills and his checkbook before beginning to write an e-mail to his girlfriend: *Dear Reena, I miss you so much. I just heard something, and I thought u might be interested. Somebody made a noise. Yelling. A scream maybe. It's funny about noises like this in the city. You fry the eggs, you listen to the radio, you check your e-mail, you go on as if nothing has happened, you*

But no: there it was again. A second scream. He put on his shoes, ran down the stairwell, and stepped outside. He turned northeast. The day presented him with brick and asphalt, scraggly warehouse-district trees, a school bus, a construction crane in the distance, the sun shining over them all. A scream—but no screamer. Another jogger passed by and frowned at him. Overhead, a large black bird was flapping around, chased by a sparrow or a starling. He couldn't tell one bird from another. Stopping for a moment, he saw a ringlet of red hair on the sidewalk, as if someone had violently yanked it out from someone else's scalp. Benny went back inside and after breakfast set off for work.

———

That night, Benny began his daily walk along the Mississippi, avoiding the park at the end of the street where he had once been mugged. He still retained a limp from being hit in the leg that time with a baseball bat. They had struck him from behind and just above the knee. He hadn't seen them. It was like being struck by God. When he had fallen forward, a large man had reached into his pocket and grabbed his wallet before Benny could twist around to see who it was. The mugger had grunted quizzically as his fingers wormed inside Benny's trouser pocket before he took what he wanted. Well, the wallet had only been a wallet. Benny had canceled the credit cards and gone to the DMV to replace his driver's license. Tonight the air above the river smelled of vegetation, a green turtle–like aroma thick with reptilian life, but despite the attractions of the watery stink, Benny did not cross the street to the sidewalk beside the river until he had passed the unlit park where demons sat coiled patiently in the shadows waiting for him.

On both sides of the Mississippi, outdated buildings with limestone foundations that once housed mills—flour and lumber and woolen mills, once the source of the city's wealth—stood in bleached floodlight like museum artifacts that no one was permitted to touch anymore.

He detoured past a coffee shop and through the front window saw his friend Elijah, a pediatrician who had moved to Minneapolis from the Bay Area a few years ago. His friend was sipping espresso and reading a copy of *City Pages* in the corner. Benny went inside.

"Doctor."

"Takemitsu." The pediatrician took another sip of his

espresso. "Funny. You don't *look* Japanese," he said automatically, for the hundredth time, peering at his newspaper. They'd been friends ever since they'd met at a Democratic-Farmer-Labor Party precinct caucus, where they'd both volunteered to be delegates to the county convention. They canvassed in their neighborhood, and on Election Day they both drove oldsters to the polls.

"What're you reading?" Benny asked.

"The sex advice column. I'm married, so it's irrelevant. How's tricks, by the way?"

"Tricks? Oh, the tricks are fine," Benny said. He sat down. "So, Doctor, you're not home again? How come you're hanging out in a downtown coffee shop at this hour? What's the appeal?" The questions were all rhetorical, a means to get conversation started. Benny knew perfectly well why his friend was sitting there.

Elijah seemed to droop for a moment. He had a heavy five o'clock shadow and bags under his eyes, and he pretended to ignore his friend. "Fuck you," he said tiredly. "I'm decompressing. Just came back from rounds at the hospital, and I'm not ready for the homecoming. I'm embittered. See me? An embittered man sits before you. Would you explain to me what got me into doctoring? I can't remember now." Benny said nothing. The doctor shook his head. "It's hard to witness, kids being sick, kids with mitochondrial disorders, kids being brave, et cetera. I feel like Ivan Karamazov or somebody like that. See how fat I'm getting?" He reached inside his coat and snapped his suspenders. "And what about you, Mr. Architect?" Elijah, his spirits visibly lifting at the prospect of irritating his friend, leaned back and finally grinned affectionately at Benny. "Did you design any big-box stores today? In one of those new beautiful Bauhaus strip malls they have now? Fluorescent lights and linoleum to remind us all of our proud humanity? Man, I do love strip malls. Incidentally, you kinda look like a vampire tonight."

"That's how you know I'm Asian. All the great vampires are Asian."

"I've noticed. Except you don't look Asian. You just look like a vampire."

"Vampires are hot."

"Benny, you sound like a girl when you say that," Elijah said, still smiling amiably.

Benny shrugged. "So I sound like a girl. Big deal. Girl vampires have it going on. Anyway, people dig sexual ambiguity. They find it attractive. And Reena likes me."

"*Likes?* What about *loves*? And she doesn't live here, does she? Your pale vampire complexion hasn't moved her to move here, I've noticed."

"We need our solitude. She doesn't . . . I don't know. She doesn't want to *commit*." He pronounced the word as if he were holding it at a distance, with a pair of tongs. "And, get this, she says she doesn't want, or like, children." The doctor shook his head in disbelief. "Which is all my mother ever wants out of me, those grandchildren. I can't do it alone. Hey," Benny said, "speaking of girls, I heard a girl screaming this morning while I was getting dressed."

"Not in your bedroom, I hope." Elijah sat up and examined Benny with a kind of doctor-expression. "And?"

"I didn't do anything until she screamed a second time. Then I ran outside. But there was no one there. Only this."

He reached into his pocket and pulled out the ringlet of red hair.

Elijah examined it. "There's something I want you to do," he said. "I want you to get rid of that."

"Why?"

"You shouldn't be carrying someone's hair around in your pocket. It's like a horror movie. 'Creepy' is I think the right word for carrying hair around in that manner."

"Okay." Benny put it back in his pocket. "When are Susan and you going to invite me to dinner again? I miss your hospitality. I miss the free meals."

"Oh, any day now, possibly when we like you again. But that hair is a kind of disincentive. *You* could invite us to dinner, you know. One of those meals? That you cook? *You* could open the door for Elijah and Susan. You could heat something up. You could make a social effort."

"Soon," Benny said. He stood up. "Soon. Doctor, I'm on my aerobic walk, and I gotta get my heart rate elevated."

Elijah gave him a dispirited goodbye wave.


Three weeks later, on his way out to his evening stroll, Benny passed two of his friends, the lesbians from down the hall, Donna and Ellie, just outside the building. They referred to themselves alphabetically as "the D and the E," and tonight they were walking their keeshonds. Engaged in conversation, they waved to him as he crossed the block. He waved back, not wanting to interrupt them. When the two women were talking together, the bond between them—heads turned in a mutual gaze, slightly bowed, the conversation quiet and slow and half-smiling—seemed more intimate than sex. Their friendship, no, their love, resembled . . . what? Prayer, or some other category that Benny didn't currently believe in.

By the time he reached the Washington Avenue Bridge across the Mississippi, he had worked up a light sweat. He planned to cross the river, turn around, and then head back. He would shower before bed and be asleep by midnight. Tonight the joggers and lovers were out in force, along with the shabby old men who held out their hands for money. A panhandle was like a scream: you never knew what was appropriate, how much help to offer, what to do.

Crossing the bridge on the pedestrian level, he counted the number of people on foot. He liked taking inventories; solid figures reassured him. About seven people were out tonight, including one guy with a backpack sprinting in Benny's direction, two people strolling, and a young woman with a vaguely studenty appearance who stood motionless, leaning against the railing and staring down at the river. The sodium lights gave them all an orange-tan tint. The young woman tapped her fingers along the guardrail, took out a cell phone, and after taking a picture of herself, dropped the phone into the river below. She licked her lips and laughed softly as the phone disappeared into the dark.

Benny stopped. Something was about to happen. As he watched, she gathered herself up and with a quick athletic movement hoisted herself over so that she was standing on the railing's other side with her arms braced on the metal-work behind her. If she released her arms and leaned forward, she would plunge down into the river. One jogger went past her without noticing what she was doing. What *was* she doing? Benny hurried toward her.

Seeing him out of the corner of her eye, she turned and smirked.

"Stop!" he commanded. "Wait. Don't!" He wasn't sure what to say. "What are you doing? Who are you?"

"I'm nobody. Who are you?"

"I'm just Benny," he said. "That's dangerous. Please. Why are you doing that?"

"No reason. For fun. A cheap thrill. I'm bungee jumping," she said. "Only without the bungee. See the cord?" She pointed down to where no cord was visible. "Just *kidding*! It's *imaginary*! Also, I've been feeling real cold behind my eyes," she said, "so I thought I'd do something exciting to heat myself up." Her speech style was oddly animated, and she seemed very pretty in a drab sort of way, like an honorable-mention beauty queen who hadn't taken proper care of herself. Something was off in the grooming department. Her long brown hair fell over her shoulders, and her T-shirt had a corporate logo and the words JUST DO IT across the front. Her eyes, when she glanced at Benny, were deep and penetrating. Her feet in sandals displayed toenails polished a bright red, so that under the streetlights they had the appearance of war paint. She gave off a shadowy gleam. "I've been feeling kind of temporary lately," she said. "How about you, *Benny*? You been feeling permanent?"

He reached out for her arm and clasped it. "Yes, I have. So. Please come back," he said.

"Fuck you doin'?" she said, laughing. "Don't harass me. Let go. Let go of me or maybe I'll actually *jump*." Irony was the new form of chastity and was everywhere these days. You never knew whether people meant what they said or whether it was all a goof.

"No," Benny said. "I don't think so. I won't let go." To his astonishment, a couple strolled past them without paying them any mind at all. He thought of crying out for help, but noise might panic this woman, startle her, inspiring her to make her move, unless she was playing a late-night prank. After all, she *was* grinning. Dear God, he thought, the perfect incongruity of that grin. He felt a sudden resolve to hold on to her forever if he had to.

"This isn't a big plan I have," she said cheerfully. "It's just a personal happening." She waited. "Don't you ever want to get on the other side of the boundary? It's so exciting over here, so lethal. It looks back at you." She waited. "So much fun. And against boredom? Boredom," she said urgently, "must be defeated."

"You shouldn't be standing there. It's a terrible idea."

"Don't be like that," she said, staring down at the river. "Okay, maybe it's a terrible idea, but it's *my* idea." Now she appeared to be sneering. She had a blue barrette in her hair. "Do you think it would take a long time to fall? What would falling feel like?" She tipped her head back. "I think it would feel like being famous. I'd laugh all the way down. I'd sign autographs."

"No. It would feel like nothing. Then like being ripped apart by water. It'd *really* hurt." He waited with his hand around her arm. He was quite strong; like everyone else he knew, he went to the gym and kept fit, and just when he had begun to consider how much she weighed and how long he'd be able to hold on to her if she leaped off the ledge and dangled there, he remembered to ask, "What's your name?"

"I won't tell you," she said. "Okay, yes, I will. It's Desdemona."

"Thanks." He moved slightly so that he was behind her, and still holding her arm, he moved his other arm so that it encircled her waist. A car honked at them. "So-called Desdemona," he said, "please come back to this side. Okay?"

"Um, no? Just leave me alone? Besides, don't you even want to get on the other side of the railing *with* me? How about some solidarity? Don't you ever want a thrill? Or a chill? Or a spill? Stop *touching* me!"

"No."

She laughed. "Such a spoilsport. Such a *square*." She twisted her head back. "You must be from around here. You smell of the Midwest."

He held on to her for another minute. Either he was trembling or she was. Finally she shook herself as if possessed by a thought. She turned around and clambered over to where Benny was standing. He released her. His heart was pounding. "Okay, I give up. Would you really have held on to me for good?" she asked. He nodded. "So that if I was dangling, you'd *keep* me? I thought so. You look sturdy. And stubborn. What's *amazing* is your investment in me, all the coins you dropped in my slot." She chattered nervously. "I'm such a dope, I really can't follow through on anything." She still hugged the railing, though on the pedestrian side, and continued to glance nervously down into the water now and then. "Did you really think I was going to jump? Would I have done that?"

"You threw away your cell phone. Anyway, I can't predict what you will or won't do. I don't know you."

"My cell phone was old. It was broken. I hated it. People kept calling me and asking me for things."

"Nevertheless," Benny said.

She twisted her head, a subtle hint of mockery in the movement. "So. It seems that the Samaritan is *not* going to go away. What do you do, Emergency Guy? I mean, Benny?"

"I'm an architect."

"An architect? Prove it." She gave him a teasing expression.

"Okay, look over there." He pointed at the art museum on the other side of the river. "That's the Weisman Art Museum. Frank Gehry designed it. He's famous. The exterior, all those bumps and bulges, are stainless-steel sheets fabricated in Kansas City, and where the museum faces the river, the design's supposed to look like a waterfall and a fish, but personally I don't think it does. I could tell you more, but that's enough."

"All right," she said. "You know who Frank Gehry is. Guess what? So do I. Anyway, I'll go home now."

"I'll walk with you."

"No, you won't."

"Yes, I will." He waited. "Otherwise you might come back here."

"Opportunist." She seemed to be estimating him, like an insurance adjuster. "If you try anything, I'll scream like a banshee. I can do that. So nothing weird, okay?"

"You're talking to me about weird?" he asked.

After walking off the bridge, they turned south into a

Somali neighborhood where men sat in erect postures at the sidewalk cafés animatedly debating, not even glancing at the two white people as they went by. A wonderful aroma seemed to be suspended in the unbreathing air, a musky cloud of coffee and chocolate and vanilla apparently imported from sub-Saharan Africa and deposited here in Minneapolis, and the atmosphere made Benny feel both provincial and ready for an adventure. The woman—he couldn't think of her as Desdemona, a joke name—had a surprisingly long and rapid stride, diving ahead of him. They turned off on a poorly lit side street into a neighborhood near a small Lutheran college, where she stopped in front of a nondescript apartment building on whose third floor, she claimed, she lived. Standing fixedly out on the sidewalk, Benny felt a shock of attraction for her, an eerie electrical charge. The attraction alarmed him. For what possible reason would she interest him? No prior cause ever explained his rogue desires, but this one maybe had to do with grieving a person who was still alive. He didn't want to leave her, that was all, and he had to think of what to say immediately.

"So, Desdemona, what do you do?" he asked.

"So, okay, it isn't Desdemona, it's Sarah, and I don't do anything important." She shrugged. He saw that her fingernails had been gnawed at. "I merely take up space. I'm one of those *little* underemployed people that you hear about. You know, one of those *my-noot* service persons. I have many degrees. I work in a day-care center where I look after the munchkins and I play the piano."

"Well, that's something. What's your last name?"

"Lemming. Kinda ironic, isn't it? What's yours?"

"Takemitsu." He braced himself for the moment when she'd say that he didn't look Japanese. Instead, she scanned his face for a quality she apparently required in a man. A moment later she slipped sideways away from close proximity to him.

"I also do stand-up comedy now and then," she said. She waited for him to laugh, and he laughed. "See? I made you crack up. That's my line. Really, Benny . . . that *is* your name, right? *Benny?*" He nodded. "You didn't really think I was going to off myself tonight, did you? Like someone in a movie?" Then she spun around, quickly touching him. "The mysteriously self-destructive and glamorous-but-funny lady on the edge of the bridge and of existence itself? And you, the brave macho rescuer? That's such a male fantasy, isn't it? Wow, for banal. Hey, are you one of those comic-book heroes? One of the Fantastic Four? Which one are you? Do I get to guess?" Without waiting for an answer, she went into her building, saying neither thank you nor goodbye.

When Benny returned to his apartment, the phone was ringing. "This ayatollah walks into a bar," the caller began. It was her. "He's got the ayatollah headdress, ayatollah beard, and ayatollah white robe, the little ayatollah sandals on his little ayatollah feet. And the bartender says, 'Whattya have?' The ayatollah says, 'Let's not rush things. First of all, which way is east?'"

The joke went on for a long time, and he laughed politely at its punch line. When she had finished it and had hung up, he stood there feeling a slow trickle of infatuation, like a poison or its antidote, dripping down onto his heart.

———

The next day, he drove by her building and dropped off a note inside her mailbox in the building's vestibule. The note asked, *May I see you?* Somehow she found out where he lived, because two days later he received a mailed letter with her return address. Inside the envelope she'd folded a single sheet of paper on which she had written *Yes*. At the bottom of the letter the signature read *Madeline Elster*. Who was Madeline Elster? One of her aliases? Desdemona, Madeline Elster—circus names. Using Internet sources, he had managed to check her out: she was Sarah Lemming, exactly as she'd claimed, and she worked at the Cedar-Riverside Little Folks Center. That evening after drinking a double Scotch, he called his girlfriend, Reena, and told her he was sorry but their thing, their arrangement, was over, and they were through as a couple. Gazing at the minute hand of his watch, he patiently listened to her inevitable sobbing questions. It's just not working, he said. *Not working,* as if they were an unemployed couple. He made his voice as vacuous as possible while she wept. You just had to wade through the tears to get to the opposing shore.

Then he called Sarah back, and they arranged to have lunch at a Mexican restaurant. On the appointed day, eating tacos, she spoke pleasantly and impersonally about her former ambitions as a musician; someday, she said, she would play Ravel and Bach for him, so that he could witness her at her best. She hadn't been able to support herself as a rehearsal pianist or as an accompanist, and she'd been stymied by her expectations of what had been promised and what actually happened. A performance degree from a midwestern university: What good was *that*? Where was the future in it? There had been no future.

Even while talking, she had a slight stoop, as if she were ducking under a door frame. She bent slightly to camouflage her attractiveness. Her posture was like an apology of sorts for her prettiness, not the demure kind that shy women tended to project, but another sort—impudent, but infected by reticence.

Neither of them mentioned how they had met. The subject no longer qualified as speakable. That temporarily desperate woman had been replaced by this one in front of him, eating tacos. This daytime Sarah conversed and was sensible about herself. But the nighttime one pestered his waking dreams. She leaned out over the river, and he saw himself reaching for her arm.

In one of his dreams, she and Benny were handcuffed to each other.

Eventually she agreed to have dinner with him, and in the weeks that followed they had other dinners, other walks. He would escort her back to her building, but she wouldn't invite him in. She talked about children and music—especially the music of Bach, comparing it to intricate God-given architecture. When nervous, she grew stylishly knowing and flippant, and nightfall intensified the effect of a nocturnal joker self emerging from the rubble of daytime. She often gave the appearance of thinking about something she would not say. On the evening when she first wore eyeliner for him, she told him that she had grown up in Connecticut horse country, had gone to college here in Minnesota and had stayed around, had been married for a few months before she and her husband had ended it amicably. She had two sisters, both very rich. One worked in an investment bank; the other had married well. Her sisters both had kids—two apiece, along with the private schools, the ballet lessons, the soccer, French and Mandarin immersion. She herself was the black sheep of the family, the artiste. She spoke of her personal history as if it were a dull annoyance.

Now, many years later, gazing at Julian and seeing a remnant of Sarah's face in the boy's characteristic skeptical expression, Benny imagines those days—including the trip to the mall and a little gag they played on a clerk—as a charade of sorts in which he was being invited to try out different roles, shedding one after another as Sarah herself did, until he might find one that suited him, although what he didn't understand at the time (as he does now, of course) is that what he mistook for a charade and a pastime, a stunt, a form of harmless amateur wickedness, was for her a tether that tied her to the Earth.

She called him a week later on a Wednesday night. "I want to play something for you," she said. "I've been practicing and practicing. I'll play it on my very own piano." For comic effect she pronounced it "pye-ano." She had never invited him into her apartment, so he felt that his patience might be rewarded at last, along with his curiosity.

After being buzzed upstairs, he saw that her door was

already open, and she stood inside with her hand on her hip. She wore jeans and a pink T-shirt and was barefoot. The trace of some perfume shielded her lightly but protectively. Her living room contained a sofa and chair and coffee table in the big-box Swedish contemporary style of assemble-it-yourself furniture. Near poverty now had a kind of opaque, cool cleanliness and an odor of sanctimony. You didn't have to sit down in cast-off wing chairs smelling of marijuana and mildew anymore, but the sparse impersonality of her living room had the quality of an emergency, as if no one had bothered to think about what should be located here or had the patience or inclination to arrange it. A few books were out. The human presence had been nearly eradicated from the room except for the scratched-up spinet piano in the corner. Other than that, the room had a claustrophobic cleanliness. Everything here seemed temporary.

"So," Benny said. "A concert? What are we privileged to hear?"

She had disappeared into the kitchen and came back out with a cold beer, which she handed to him. He could tell that she had an agenda that included whatever she was about to play.

"So," she said. "I've been working on this piece. It's called 'Ondine' and it's from this composer's, Ravel's, group of pieces *Gaspard de la Nuit*. There's a story behind it. Do you want to hear the story?" Benny nodded, although he already knew the story. He had been a keyboard musician, and, though he'd never been capable of playing this particular piece, he knew about it. "So: Ondine is a water sprite. She's very pale and intriguing. Seductive, too. She appears to the poet and she offers him a ring—a ring! how about *that?*—and she also offers him the kingdom of the waters although, duh, he can't live there because he doesn't have gills. Anyway, the poet tells her that he loves a mortal woman, so Ondine gets upset and jealous and angry, and she sulks. So like a woman, right? After she's finished crying, she laughs and disappears in a shower of droplets on the windowpane. The point is, he can't have her."

Benny nodded and took a swig of the beer.

Sarah sat down at the piano and put both of her bare feet on the pedals. She started to play. The piece was in seven sharps, C-sharp major, and it began softly, starting with a rumbling swift shower of thirty-second notes. Around the third bar, Ondine comes out, sweet and expressive, calling him to her. Sarah's hands sped over the keys as she followed the score, and Benny got up from the sofa and went over to where she sat to turn the page for her.

She stopped playing. "What? You can read music?" He nodded. She started up again, unhappily scowling. The piece was showy and fantastically difficult, and from her approximations he could tell that she was a very good but not a first-rate pianist who was just slopping her way through it, energized by the former musical ambitions she wished to put on display. Also, he saw that she wanted to show off. She made some clumsy mistakes but bushwhacked to the end, Benny standing beside her, turning the pages.

When she finished, he put down his beer and clapped. "Jeez," he said. "That was great. You're terrific."

"You liked it?" she asked shyly. She wouldn't smile. She waited, looking straight ahead at the last page of the score.

"I loved it."

"Really?"

"Yes."

"You're not flattering me?"

"No, I don't think so," he said. White lies didn't cost you much in the short term.

"I made a lot of mistakes. When did you ever play the piano?" she asked.

"Junior high. High school. College. I was all right. I was in a few bands. But I couldn't play like that."

"Benny," she said. His hand rested on her shoulder. He didn't quite know how it had gotten there. "Benny," she repeated. "*Benjamin*. Here's the deal. I know you want me, and I know you've been patient with me, and I want you to know that I have feelings for you, too."

"It's more than that," he said. "I—"

"Don't say it," she interrupted. "You can tell me later if you want to. But first I have to tell you something. You would like to make love to me, I know, and I would like that too. It would be good to have you in my bed, and not just as an occasional visitor. But there are two conditions."

Whenever he told this story, as he did to Elijah one night several weeks later, Benny would stop here. Some stories, he felt, you should never repeat. If you do tell them, a trust is violated. But this story had become so bacterial that he had to pass its contagion on to others who might help him bear it. He'd become incapable of carrying it around alone. Besides, Elijah was a doctor.

"So?" Elijah asked. "What were the conditions she gave you?" Benny squirmed. "Come on, Benny, out with it. I've heard everything by now. Confess."

"Well, they weren't that big," Benny said.

"Out with it."

"I couldn't kiss her," Benny admitted. "That was the first condition. We could make love, but I couldn't ever kiss her on the lips. Anywhere else, fine. On the lips, no. She said she was phobic about it. She couldn't help it, she said."

"And did you agree to this?" the doctor asked.

"Yes, but I gave her a condition of my own."

"Why'd you do that?"

"Because women shouldn't be the only ones to set the conditions. Men should be able to set conditions, too. You can't just cave in on everything if you're negotiating. I agree with feminism but I need a place to stand. Anyway, I told her I wanted her to color her hair. I told her that I wanted her hair to be red. I was forceful on the subject."

"You did? That's messed up. What did she say?"

"She said, 'Sure.'"

"Did she ask you why? Did you show her that red hair of yours from the sidewalk? I certainly hope not. Please tell me you didn't do that. What was the other condition?"

"She wanted me to design a house she could be happy in. Just a sketch would do. I told her I would try."

"A house? So you were agreeable to all this? What happened then?"

"We made love, sort of. Until then I had never made love without starting with the kisses. I mean, a person can do it. You can have sex without kissing on the lips. Ever seen porn?" Elijah gravely nodded. "They don't kiss much in porn, do they? Well, this was like that."

"Yeah, but how did it feel?"

"I don't know. Beautiful. Lonely. Sweet. Distant. Remote. It was what I wanted in a way I didn't want it. God, I can't say. Like she was guarding her soul or something."

"I really hate to tell you this, Benny, but I think the, uh, really obvious thing is that she doesn't love you. She'd *like* to, she really would, and she's been working at it, but she can't. The nonkissing is the big clue. If I were you, I'd get out now. *Finita la commedia* is my advice. Oh, and did she color her hair?"

"Yeah," Benny said. "It's beautiful. Listen: I think she might love me someday, only she can't say so. And there's this one other thing."

"Another *thing*. I can't stand it. Which is?"

"She's gotten herself a stand-up gig. Did I mention this already? She's going to be at the Longfellow Comedy Club a few weeks from now. Two nights, Friday and Saturday. I've never heard her do stand-up. She says she's done it for years but not lately. She's been working on it."

"You better watch out. She's going to get up onstage and tell everybody you have a small dick, and they'll all laugh."

"No, she won't. First of all, I don't have that, and second of all, she wouldn't."

"Wait and see."

"Maybe you should come out and witness it. Would you do that?"

"Depends. I might drop by if I don't have rounds. Or child care. Or obligations to Susan. Or house repair. I'm a busy fellow." He sat up. "After all, I am a *married man*. And I am a *physician*. I am a *citizen*. I have multiple responsibilities." Elijah's cell phone rang as if on cue. He checked the screen but did not answer it.

"Then why are you here?" Benny waved his hand to indicate the coffee shop where they both sat. "If you're so busy, why are you here?"

"Have you slept with her again?" Elijah asked. "Have you two become lovers?" He waited. "I don't mean to pry." He smiled at his own hypocrisy.

"Yes," Benny said. "Yes, we have slept together again. And no, we have not become lovers. Not really." He bunched up a paper napkin and threw it in the wastebasket. "At least *she* hasn't. Because I told her that I was falling in love with her. I got out on a limb."

"And what did she say?"

"She said, 'Well, I can't say the same.'"


Sometimes when Benny sat on the barren furniture in Sarah's apartment, he could hear her in the bathroom, the door closed, practicing her comedy routine. She kept her voice down to a rushed murmuring followed by exclamations. She practiced her stage laugh, a prompt to the audience. When she eventually came out to the living room, he volunteered to listen to her monologue, but she always said no, she had to keep it to herself for a while.

He didn't know her after all, he decided. He lay awake staring at the ceiling while Sarah slept beside him. They had everything except intimacy. Maybe you could get along without that. She seemed to think so. All the same, he believed she loved him somehow. Earlier that day, she had called him up at work and in a breathless voice told him that she had made the greatest discovery—no one had thought of it before, but now *she* had. "Think of a dog," she said. "Okay, now suppose you have a really smart dog. Let's say you have a border collie. Dogs don't get much smarter than that, do they? I don't think so. A border collie can do anything a dog can do. They can herd sheep, they can recognize words, they can save children from storm drains during flood season. But suppose you try to explain the planet Mars to a border collie. The dog is smart, all right, but nothing in the dog brain can accommodate the idea of Mars, can it? No. The dog can never ever understand that there's a planet beyond ours called Mars. Mars will never register in its cranium. A dog can't think a single thought about Mars." She waited for this aperçu to sink in. "It's not the dog's fault. Okay, so now suppose that we have limitations on our brains, like the limitation on a dog brain. And you know what we can't get, ever?"

"I don't know," Benny said at his drawing desk, blueprints spread out in front of him.

"Exactly," Sarah said with triumph. "*You don't know*. And you never will. But here's what I believe: I believe that because of the way we're all wired up, we'll never know God, *and that's just for starters*. Something is out there, but we'll never have any concept of what it is. All we have are these dumb fairy tales about crucified guys with beards and dead people coming alive again and the book sealed with seven seals. Also, by the way, we'll never know the actual structure of the universe. And there's something else we'll never know. Or, at least, *you'll* never know it. And I'll never know it."

"What's that?" Benny asked.

"You'll never know me." Sarah laughed. "And I'll never know you."

Benny waited, his heart thumping in his chest, in a state of mind that he would describe as "desolate" the next time he saw Elijah, even though Elijah would try to shake him out of it by calling it a girl-word that only girls would use.

"Is that so bad?" she asked. "I don't think that's so bad!" She paused, and when Benny said nothing, she said, "I've hurt your feelings, haven't I?" Her voice sounded heartbreakingly cheerful. "We're all planets," she said, "and we're all covered with clouds, Benny, which, in my opinion, in my dog brain, is what liberates us."

To Benny, she didn't sound saved, but just then the sun emerged from behind a tree outside his office window, and he remembered to say, "Sarah, I love you, and I have to go."


On architectural paper he drew a Prairie-style house for her, then discarded it. (Too dark.) Then he tried out a post-Bauhaus horizontal-and-vertical glass house in the Philip Johnson style, but the windows made it too exposed to the gaze of the outdoors. She wouldn't like that. He tried a monumental bunker that would call for poured concrete. How cold it seemed! Finally he drew a little A-frame cabin in the woods beside a lake, though he wondered whether such a home might be too isolated for her.

No one had ever asked him to design a house in which a

human being might be happy. It was an architectural koan, he decided, meant to tie him into a comical knot.

On the way to the Longfellow Comedy Club, one month later, with Benny driving the car, Sarah showed no trace of jumpiness or excitement. She sat quietly settled on the passenger side. Benny didn't know what the protocols were about talking to your girlfriend on the way to her comedy set, so he didn't say much, worrying that if he did speak up, he would give away the miasmic dread that had gradually settled itself over him. "You look great," he told her glumly, and she nodded. She had girled herself up and had applied a shellac of glamour: she'd worn her best punk T-shirt and jeans, her scuffed saddle shoes, and her red hair had been sprayed into a stylish disorder. Over the hair she wore a battered attitude hat tinted green like some ghastly Irish shrub. "Are you nervous?"

"Nervous? No." She was texting someone on her phone and didn't look up.

"I'd be nervous."

"Yes, you would be." She nodded, agreeing with herself. Autumn had arrived, and the streets swirled with fallen leaves, some of which stuck to the windshield. Before long, he thought, the snow will be in the air.

"The snow will be in the air soon," Sarah said, giving voice to his thoughts in that eerie way she sometimes had.

"Remind me of when your set begins," he said, although he already knew.

"Ten. By the way, Benny, if I mention you, don't take it personally, okay?"

"Okay."

"It's just a comedy act."

"Right."

"Remember that."

The Longfellow was located between two city lakes, Hiawatha and Nokomis, and out in front a line of elegantly scruffy patrons stood waiting to get in. The poet's face, with its silver hair and silver beard painted on a signboard above the entrance, was outlined with neon tubing, a joke-optic. Underneath the neon, the club's name had been lettered in Braggadocio font.

## THE LONGFELLOW
## A comedy club

After they parked, Benny said, "Good luck," and he leaned over to peck Sarah's cheek.

"Thanks. Sit in the front row," she said. "Laugh for me." Before getting out of the car, she touched him tenderly on his face. "You're a good man," she said in a whisper. "Sometimes that's enough." Then she disappeared through the club's back entrance.

After waiting in line and paying the admission price—Sarah hadn't given him a comp—Benny located himself as close as he could to the stage, where he was surrounded by men and women in camouflage gear, sunglasses, leather vests, caps with the visors reversed, faded jeans, and ripped T-shirts advertising defunct Internet start-ups. These kids had bypassed glitz and gone straight to hyperirony: to his left, a woman with purple streaks in her hair sported a tattoo on her arm: I'M FOR SALE. A genial and loudmouthed clown-army, they quieted when the emcee came out and introduced the leadoff, a skinny kid in a Mets baseball hat who stood absolutely still on the stage and said that he suffered from autism. His name, he said, was Joe Autism. For ten minutes he provided an autism-based commentary in an absentminded monotone. "What if elevators wanted to go sideways?" he asked. He waited, and the silence became comically tense.

Benny zoned out. He may have dozed off, because when he opened his eyes, the emcee had introduced Sarah, and she was out onstage.

"Hello, Longfellow," she crowed, and the audience woofed and hooted. "I'm Sarah. Sarah Lemming. I throw myself off things. I'm suicidal. Anybody here suicidal? Ladies?" Many women in the audience clapped and cheered. "Yeah, I thought so. No shame *there*. None at all. A few in every crowd. But it's *so* fuckin' hard, 'cause rescue-squad types are always trying to *stop* you." She held on to the microphone and paced menacingly back and forth on the narrow stage. "I *hate* that. Guys are always trying to *save* you. All you guys practicing your superhero moves? What the fuck is *that*?" She appeared befuddled. "Relapse and have a beer. And then there's the *actual* damn superheroes! I am so tired of Spider-Man— a real asshole, can I say that without being sued?—and that other guy, the famous one in the blue tights and the red cape, grabbing me and feeling me up. And flying around! They think it'll impress you, being airborne, dodging 727s. But it really just musses your hair and gives you vertigo. *Leave me alone, superheroes,* okay? Let me go. Let me fall splat on the pavement. Rescue someone else, for a change. My therapist disagrees. My therapist said I should *vote for life*." She stopped to glare at the audience. "She says life is better than death because you can still go shopping as long as you're not dead. Wise words! Words of wisdom. She's quoting Socrates, I think. Or Pluto or somebody. I'm trying to remember that wisdom. I mean, if Bed Bath & Beyond isn't the meaning of life, come up right here onstage and tell me: What is? Yeah, my boyfriend saved me the last time. What's-his-name in the blue tights didn't show up. The famous superhero had another appointment in Metropolis with Lex Luthor or Eradicator, so this guy did it. A passerby. He saved me. He *became* my boyfriend. He's in the audience. Give him a hand." Everyone applauded. "Yeah, he didn't ask much in return, either. He just wanted me to fuck him. So I did. What's the harm in that? A mere favor. He's scared I'm going to make fun of him and say in front of everybody that he has a little dick. Naw, he has a big friendly dick. That's why I don't mind the mold in his bathroom. Am I right, ladies?" More cheers. "Yes, it's true: he and I have sex. He loves me. He saves lives. A hero, right? I'm not afraid to admit it. We get in bed and that thing happens where you open your legs and he puts that probe in there that guys have. What you don't plan on are the unexpected consequences." Just then, her cell phone rang. She fished it out of her pocket, looked at the screen, and said to the audience, "Excuse me." She put the phone to her ear. "Hello? Oh, great!" She closed the phone, grinned, and put it back. She must have timed the call somehow to ring a few minutes into the set. "Those were the results from the lab. Guess what? I'm pregnant!"

The audience gasped, laughed, and applauded. Benny felt himself going very still.

"Yup," she said, "I'm knocked up. Anybody here ever been knocked up? Guys?" A few hip men applauded. "Ladies?" More applause. "Well, it happens. The injection of man-goop causes it. That's what they tell me. That reminds me of a story. Two pregnant women, one smart and the other stupid, are sitting on a park bench. The first one, the smart one, turns to the second and says, 'Well, here we are, both pregnant.' The second one nods. The smart one leans back. 'How'd it happen? I certainly ask myself that question. With me,' she says, 'and my husband, Sam—well, he can't keep his hands off me. He wants to make love morning, noon, and night. He's wearing me out. I'm sore all the time. I hardly have energy to work on my postdoc. Maybe when I'm in my third trimester, he'll stop.' The second woman, the stupid one, nods. 'You think *you* got it bad?' she says. 'My guy, Freddy, he can't never get it up. Also he don't like to touch me, neither.' The first woman looks over. 'So how'd you get yourself in the family way?' she asks. Second woman pats her stomach and says, 'Oh, this one here's on account of the milkman.' The first woman says, 'The milkman?' The second woman says, 'Yeah. He comes by to make his delivery every Tuesday.

He's got this nice red convertible sports car, and he's wearing Old Spice, and he always gives me a pound of butter after he's fucked me.' First woman says, 'He doesn't sound like an actual milkman. With a convertible? I never heard of that.' Second woman says, 'Oh, he's a milkman all right. And he dresses like they all do—ten-gallon hat, bolo tie, and alligator shoes. And also, ask yourself, *"If he ain't a real milkman, where'd he get the butter?"'"*

She continued her set for another five minutes. When she finished, the applause and cheering were loud. People stood up: she'd been a great success. There was general acclaim. Benny turned around while everyone clapped. He saw Elijah sitting in the back of the club, gazing back at him accusingly, as one would gaze at a collaborator.

After making his way out of a side exit, Benny walked toward his car. Inside, behind the wheel, he leaned back and closed his eyes. He groaned. In the inner circle of Hell, he thought, Satan is telling jokes. He's sitting on his throne cracking up. They're all guffawing down there in the fiery pit.

Finally she entered the car. "You didn't come backstage," she said. "How come? Goddamn! They *loved* me. You didn't congratulate me." She looked over at his ravaged face. "What happened to you?" She reached over to him without touching him. "Have you been crying?"

"Sarah," he said. "Are you really pregnant?"

"Yup! I wanted to surprise you. Isn't it great? Aren't you happy? Surprised?"

"Well, yes. Surprised. That's one word. But we used condoms!"

"Oh, forget that. With immaculate conceptions, it's like sunlight through stained glass."

"All right. But, hey, *what is wrong with you*? Talking about me as part of your act? And what do we do now? Are we having this baby? What happens now?"

"What do you mean?"

"What d'you mean, what do I mean? What sort of person announces to her boyfriend that she's pregnant as part of a stand-up monologue in a comedy club?"

She tilted her head, smiled her Kewpie doll–like smile, and pointed her index fingers at her face. "This sort of person. That's who."

"In that case, we're going somewhere."

"Where?"

He simply shook his head as he started the car and drove north toward the center of the city, past windblown gesticulating trees and nighttime blue-tinted rain. "Aren't you going to tell me how great I was onstage?" she asked finally, staring out at the blurred houses passing on her side of the car. Inside those houses, ordinary lovers were curled up, sleeping together. Now he was speeding in a nocturnal and correct manner, or so he felt; you can always speed with impunity if no one else is up and around, if no one else is awake, if you are sober and number yourself among the last ones.

"You were great onstage," he replied, his voice drained of color.

She closed her eyes, appearing to doze, having shaken off her excitement and entered the exhaustion that follows, and when she opened them again, he had parked the car near a university structure on the west bank of the river, and he was helping her out of the passenger side, and with his right arm around her and his right hand grasping her elbow, he escorted her down toward the Washington Avenue Bridge over the Mississippi. She seemed to be half-conscious, her gait like that of a sleepwalker. She probably thought she was dreaming this night, this walk.

"What's that song lyric? 'It's infinitely late at night'?"

"Oh, no," Benny said. "It's much later than that. Here we are."

She opened her eyes suddenly, and when she did, she seemed to come totally into consciousness and to realize their location. "Jesus, this? Here? What's this about?"

"Yes, here." This was where they had first met. "Look down." She followed his instruction. Below them, water flowed in the indifferent darkness, sovereign in its shadowy blankness. "Pretty funny, right? Your phone is down there in the water. Well, here we are, sweetheart. Here's where I found you. And here's where I can drop you off again if you want."

"No."

"No? I got it wrong? How do I get you right, Sarah? Anyway, here's your big chance. Isn't this what you asked for? Go ahead, honey. You want to jump? I just want what you want. Go ahead." His face was a solid mask, though he wept.

"It's a long way down," she whispered.

"The longest."

They both stood looking at the river beneath them. No walkers or strollers or joggers passed behind them, and Benny couldn't hear sounds of traffic. The entire city had seemingly emptied out, and stillness possessed it, as it would a necropolis. He thought he heard his own watch ticking for two minutes before she said, "No. I can't. I'd like to, but I can't."

"You can't?" he asked. "Why not?"

For answer, she turned to him, and with one hand at his waist, she raised her other hand to Benny's face in a slow-motion caress, the most personal gesture she had ever made in his direction. "Because of you," she said. It had killed her to say it, he knew, but she had said it, and now tears were in her eyes as well. Then she whispered, "I'm a kidder. I joke about things. That's the one thing I'm serious about, my joking. That's how I meet the payroll." She was touching him here and there. "What do we do about the hopes? The loans? The, uh, ambitions? Tell me something. Are you in love with me?"

"Yes," he said miserably and proudly. "I am. I've said so. I've told you. Often."

"Okay. We'll have to work this out, I guess. But you can't stop me from what I am. I'm a joker, all right? Give me *me*."

"That was a very impressive speech," he said with pride and tenderness.

"I thought so," she said, closing her eyes. "It was me at my best."

"Could I say something else?" he asked. "Because I'll say it anyway."

"Permission to speak."

"The baby won't be laughable. Infant care ditto. Okay, so: here's my thinking. One: I still love you. Two: what are we going to do about this baby, assuming you keep it? And three: I've forgotten what three is."

"Oh, my sister called."

"What?"

"My sister, the second one, the rich wife who lives in Dutchess County?—she called. On the phone. Carrie. She's named Carrie. That's her name. That's how she was baptized. You remember Carrie? Of course you do. She's one of my two evil sisters, both of whom live in palazzos. She said she'll take the baby if we want her to." Sarah paused. "She'd be happy to acquire him, her, it. She's used to mergers and acquisitions. She and her husband, Lord Randolph, have these amazing pots of money. Their dragon wings are spread out wide over their vast illegal fortune wrested out of the hands of the poor and harmless. Randolph participates in a cartel of international slime. One more baby will hardly make a dent in their studied concentration on cash."

"You called her? You *told* her? And she made an offer? No, she won't do that."

"You're right, she won't," Sarah said. "And do you know why?"

"Because we're going to get married?"

"Exactly! Bingo! We're going to get married. What a nice proposal. Where's my diamond ring?" Against the odds, she embraced him and held him, and then she turned so that her back was pressed against his chest, and his arms circled her waist.

"Your ring's around here somewhere. And how will our marriage work out?" he asked.

"Wait and see," she said. "I repeat: you don't know me as well as you think you do."

Which is how Benny Takemitsu, a third-generation Japanese-American who spoke little or no Japanese, a citizen of Minneapolis, Minnesota, and a journeyman architect at the firm of Byrum and Haddam, a man who had such a weakness for women who could make him laugh that he could not help falling in love with such a woman, came to marry someone who had never kissed him but who had, at least, caressed his face. They conceived a child together and still she could not bear to kiss him, not before or after the child was born, a son whom they named Julian. *Stranger things have happened,* Benny would sometimes say to himself, about his wife's particular form of chastity.

Sarah had laughed and groaned during the pains of labor to the consternation of the attending nurses, who had never witnessed such laughter before, or so much of it.

The baby's pediatrician was Dr. Elijah Elliott Jones, who praised the boy's health and equanimity and handsome features as if Julian were his own son.

Sometimes during the summer they sat together on a playground near the Mississippi River, the four of them: Benny, Sarah, Julian, and Benny's mother, Dorothea, who usually watched the baby whenever Sarah fell into one of her periodic brown studies, which, following the birth, had increased in duration and intensity. Often they packed sandwiches for a picnic, Sarah's favorite being curried chicken salad and deviled eggs. At such times, having finished nursing her son and having tied the loops of his sun hat, Sarah would stare off in the direction of the river's other shore as if Sirens sang over there, and only nudges and direct address could call her back. "She's just woolgathering," Benny's mother would say, quietly and affectionately, with a shrug, about her red-haired daughter-in-law. "In my generation," Dorothea whispered to her son, "women often looked like that. We were distracted. All of us."

Once in late summer, however, Sarah startled to life and waved her hand in front of her face to dispel the mosquitoes. She seemed to be coming up from some depth somewhere in another life. Turning one by one to Benny, Julian, and her mother-in-law, she smiled as if she approved of all of them and could bless them. Benny sat on a bench next to her, the baby sleeping in his lap, and Benny's mother, who had strolled to the edge of the Mississippi, was examining the wildflowers along the bank. Grade-school children yelled from the play structure, and nearby a freight train rattled over the river, heading north. Overhead, an airplane left behind a thin vapor trail, and in the trees the cicadas chirred. "I never played any Bach for you," she said, her voice a soft murmur. "And I don't do stand-up anymore."

"You still can."

"I've never played any Bach for you," she repeated. "I always meant to. Do you know that story about Bach? The last night of his life?" Benny shook his head. Holding Benny's hand, Sarah continued with the story. "I read it on the back of a record album. You know Bach went blind? He had cataracts and things, probably. And to make matters worse, he was treated by this guy, this traveling English quack doctor named Taylor. Goodbye, eyesight. So anyway, on the evening before he died, Bach is granted a momentary miraculous return of his vision. His sons take him outside, one on each arm, and, guess what, Bach gazes upward to see the stars. The next day he died." She looked straight up as if in imitation.

"I like that story."

"Me too." She held up her index finger to make a final pronouncement, one that Benny would always remember. "To his servant Bach, God granted a final glimpse of the heavens."

Julian, now awake in his father's lap, reached up to his mother's face, whereupon she smiled.


She didn't die the way Benny thought she would, after a long life. Instead, she lost control of her car in a rainstorm. Her car skidded off the freeway and rolled four times down a hill. She would have survived the accident if she had been wearing a seat belt, but for some reason she hadn't bothered to attach it that particular day.


After she died, he grieved for her as he had grieved for her when she had still been alive—as a passion thriving on an absence that feeds on itself year after year. For months, out of habit, he continued to sketch possible houses in which she might have been happy, although none of these houses ever had human figures inside them.

Benny's second wife, Jane, also an architect, is a tall brainy woman who loves Benny and Julian dearly, and together they have had two more children, twins. Myths and fairy tales instruct us that the arrival of the stepmother is to be feared, but she has always treated Julian as her own child, and although she has learned to discipline him when the situation requires it, her scolding lacks a certain force and confidence. One coincidence, if it could be called that, is that Jane's red hair is so similar to the color that Sarah imported to herself that the two women might have once been mistaken for each other, and when she dresses Julian in his snowsuit—actually, he's too old for that now, he can put on his own snowsuit—she and Julian talk together like co-conspirators who have known each other forever. Jane's red hair bounces behind her as she walks down the sidewalk to the school bus stop, hand in hand with her stepson, while Benny watches them both from the window.

On their free nights when they've arranged for a baby-sitter, Benny and Jane go dancing, her particular hobby. He has mastered most of the ballroom steps. When they tango, he drags her passionately across the studio floor. They stare into each other's eyes, glowering with the formalized lust that their tango instructor demands. In Jane's arms Benny has gained a kind of manly confidence. Also, Jane loves kisses. "Mommy kisses *a lot*," Julian has observed with affectionate irritability, wiping his face off boy-style after having had another Jane-kiss planted on his cheek or forehead. Her one deficit—a small one—is that she cannot make Benny laugh, and so she never tries. Besides, Julian, a boyish image of Sarah, has already grasped the essentials to being the class clown, and he has learned how to entertain his twin brothers and reduce them to giggles. Whenever Benny sees Julian laughing, his mind fogs over a bit. Julian may grow up to be a joker and a troublemaker, but Benny no longer tries to imagine his oldest son's future, and in any case, what Julian might do in life is, as people say, another story altogether.

# Charity

## 1.

He had fallen into bad trouble. He had worked in Ethiopia for a year—teaching in a school and lending a hand at a medical clinic. He had eaten all the local foods and been stung by the many airborne insects. When he'd returned to the States, he'd brought back an infection—the inflammation in his knees and his back and his shoulders was so bad that sometimes he could hardly stand up. Probably a viral arthritis, his doctor said. It happens. Here: have some painkillers.

Borrowing a car, he drove down from Minneapolis to the Mayo Clinic, where after two days of tests the doctors informed him that they would have no firm diagnosis for the next month or so. Back in Minneapolis, through a friend of a friend, he visited a wildcat homeopathy treatment center known for traumatic-pain-relief treatments.

The center, in a strip-mall storefront claiming to be a weight loss clinic (*weight no more*), gave him megadoses of meadowsweet, a compound chemically related to aspirin. After two months without health insurance or prescription coverage, he had emptied his bank account, and he gazed at the future with shy dread.

Through another friend of a friend, he managed to get his hands on a few superb prescription painkillers, the big ones, gifts from heaven. With the aid of these pills, he felt like himself again. He blessed his own life. He cooked some decent meals; he called his boyfriend in Seattle; he went around town looking for a job; he made plans to get himself to the Pacific Northwest. When the drugs ran out and the pain returned, worse this time, like being stabbed in his knees and shoulders, along with the novelty of addiction's chills and fevers, the friend of a friend told him that if he wanted more pills at the going street rate, he had better go see Black Bird. He could find Black Bird at the bar of a club, The Lower Depths, on Hennepin Avenue. "He's always there," the friend of a friend said. "He's there now. He reads. The guy sits there studying Shakespeare. Used to be a scholar or something. Pretends to be a Native American, one of those impostor types. Very easy to spot. I'll tell him you're coming."

The next Wednesday, he found Black Bird at the end of The Lower Depths bar near the broken jukebox and the sign for the men's room. The club's walls had been built from limestone and rust-red brick and sported no decorative motifs of any kind. If you needed decorations around you when you drank, you went somewhere else. The peculiar orange lighting was so dim that Quinn couldn't figure out how Black Bird could read at all.

Quinn approached him gingerly. Black Bird's hair went down to his shoulders. The gray in it looked as if it had been applied with chalk. He wore bifocals and moved his finger down the page as he read. Nearby was a half-consumed bottle of 7UP.

"Excuse me. Are you Black Bird?"

Without looking up, the man said, "Why do you ask?"

"I'm Quinn." He held out his hand. Black Bird did not take it. "My friend Morrow told me about you."

"Ah-huh," Black Bird said. He glanced up with an impatient expression before returning to his book. Quinn examined the text. Black Bird was reading *Othello,* the third act.

"Morrow said I should come see you. There's something I need."

Black Bird said nothing.

"I need it pretty bad," Quinn said, his hand trembling inside his pocket. He wasn't used to talking to people like this. When Black Bird didn't respond, Quinn said, "You're reading *Othello.*" Quinn had acquired a liberal arts degree from a college in Iowa, where he had majored in global political solutions, and he felt that he had to assert himself. "The handkerchief. And Iago, right?"

Black Bird nodded. "This isn't *College Bowl,*" he said dismissively. With his finger stopped on the page, he said, "What do you want from me?"

Quinn whispered the name of the drug that made him feel human.

"What a surprise," said Black Bird. "Well, well. How do I know that you're not a cop? You a cop, Mr. Quinn?"

"No."

"Because I don't know what you're asking me or what you're talking about. I'm a peaceful man sitting here reading this book and drinking this 7UP."

"Yes," Quinn said.

"You could always come back in four days," Black Bird said. "You could always bring some money." He mentioned a price for a certain number of painkillers. "I have to get the ducks in a row."

"That's a lot of cash," Quinn said. Then, after thinking it over, he said, "All right." He did not feel that he had many options these days.

Black Bird looked up at him but with an expression devoid of interest or curiosity.

"Do you read, Mr. Quinn?" he asked. "Everybody should read something. Otherwise we all fall down into the pit of ignorance. Many are down there. Some people fall in it forever. Their lives mean nothing. They should not exist." Black Bird spoke these words in a bland monotone.

"I don't know what to read," Quinn told him, his legs shaking.

"Too bad," Black Bird said. "Next time you come here, bring a book. I need proof you exist. The Minneapolis Public Library is two blocks away. But if you come back, bring the money. Otherwise, there's no show."


Quinn was living very temporarily in a friend's basement in Northeast Minneapolis. His parents, in a traditional old-world gesture, had disowned him after he had come out, so he couldn't call on them for support. They had uttered several unforgettable verdicts about his character, sworn they would never see him again, and that was that.

He had a sister who lived in Des Moines with a husband and two children. She did not like what she called Quinn's "sexual preferences" and had a tendency to hang up on him. None of his friends from high school had any money he could borrow; the acquaintance in whose basement he was staying was behind on his rent; and Quinn's boyfriend in Seattle, a field rep for a medical supply company, had a thing about people borrowing money. He might break up with Quinn if Quinn asked him for a loan. He could be prickly, the boyfriend, and the two of them were still on a trial basis anyway. They had met in Africa and had fallen in love over there. The love might not travel if Quinn brought up the subject of debts or his viral arthritis and inflammation or the drug habit he had recently acquired.

Now that the painkillers had run out, a kind of groggy unfocused physical discomfort had become Quinn's companion day and night. He lived in the house that the pain had designed for him. The Mayo Clinic had not called him back, and the meadowsweet's effect was like a cup of water dropped on a house fire. Sometimes the pain started in Quinn's knees and circled around Quinn's back until it located itself in his shoulders, like exploratory surgery performed using a Swiss Army knife. He had acquired the jitters and a runny nose and a swollen tongue and cramps. He couldn't sleep and had diarrhea. He was a mess, and the knowledge of the mess he had become made the mess worse. The necessity of opiates became a supreme idea that forced out all the other ideas until only one thought occupied Quinn's mind: *Get those painkillers.* He didn't think he was a goner yet, though.

He could no longer tell his dreams from his waking life. The things around him began to take on the appearance of stage props made from cardboard. Other people—pedestrians— looked like shadow creatures giving off a stinky perfume.

In the basement room where he slept, there was, leaning

against the wall, a baseball bat, a Louisville Slugger, and one night after dark, in a dreamlike hallucinatory fever, he took it across the Hennepin Avenue Bridge to a park along the Mississippi, where he hid hotly shivering behind a tree until the right sort of prosperous person walked by. Quinn felt as if he were under orders to do what he was about to do. The man he chose wore a T-shirt and jeans and seemed fit but not so strong as to be dangerous, and, after rushing out from the shadows, Quinn hit him with the baseball bat in the back of his legs. He had aimed for the back of the legs so he wouldn't shatter the guy's kneecaps. When Quinn's victim fell down, Quinn reached into the man's trouser pocket and pulled out his wallet and ran away with it, dropping the Slugger into the river as he crossed the bridge.

Back in his friend's basement, Quinn examined the wallet's contents. His hands were trembling again, and he couldn't see properly, and he wasn't sure he was awake, but he could make out that the name on the driver's license was Benjamin Takemitsu. The man didn't look Japanese in the driver's license photo, but Quinn didn't think much about it until he'd finished counting the cash, which amounted to $321, an adequate sum for a few days' relief. At that point he gazed more closely at the photo and saw that Takemitsu appeared to be intelligently thoughtful. What had he done to this man? Familiar pain flared behind Quinn's knees and in his neck, punishment he recognized that he deserved, and the pain pushed out everything else.

He called his boyfriend in Seattle. In a panic he told him that he had robbed someone named Benjamin Takemitsu, that he had used a baseball bat. The boyfriend said, "You've had a bad dream, Matty. That didn't happen. You would never do such a thing. Go back to sleep, sweetheart, and I'll call you tomorrow."

After that he lay awake wondering what had become of the person he had once been, the one who had gone to Africa. To the ceiling, he said, "I am no longer myself." He did not know who this new person was, the man whom he had become, but when he finally fell asleep, he saw in his dream one of those shabby castoffs with whom you wouldn't want to have any encounters, any business at all, someone who belonged on the sidewalk with a cardboard sign that read HELP ME. The man was crouched behind a tree in the dark, peering out with feverish eyes. His own face was the face of the castoff.

Somehow he would have to make it up to Benjamin Takemitsu.


In The Lower Depths, when Quinn entered, Black Bird did not look up. He was seated in his usual place, and once again his finger was traveling down the page. *Cymbeline* this time, a play that Quinn had never read.

"It's you," Black Bird said.

"Yes," Quinn said.

"Did you bring a book of your own?"

"No."

"All right," Black Bird said. "I can't say I'm surprised." He then issued elaborate instructions to Quinn about where in the men's room to put the money and when he, Black Bird, would retrieve it. The entire exchange took over half an hour, though the procedure hardly seemed secret or designed to fool anyone. When Quinn finally returned to his basement room, he had already gulped down two of the pills, and his relief soon grew to a great size. He felt his humanity restored until his mottled face appeared before him in the bathroom mirror, and then he realized belatedly what terrible trouble he was in.

Two days later he disappeared.

# 2.

That was as far as I got whenever I tried to compose an account of what happened to Matty Quinn—my boyfriend, my soul mate, my future life—the man who mistakenly thought I was a tightwad. I *was* very thrifty in Ethiopia, convinced that Americans should not spend large sums in front of people who owned next to nothing. But to Matty I would have given anything. Upon his return to Minneapolis he had called me up and texted and e-mailed me with these small clues about the medical ordeal he was going through, and I had not understood; then he had called to say that he had robbed this Takemitsu, and I had not believed him. Then he disappeared from the world, from his existence and mine.

Two weeks later the investigating officer in the Minneapolis Police Department (whom I had contacted in my desperation) told me that I could certainly come to survey the city if I wished to. After all, this Officer Erickson said, nothing is stopping you from trying to find your friend, although I understand that your permanent home is in Seattle and you do not know anyone here. It's a free country, so you're welcome to try. However, circumstances being what they are, I wouldn't get your hopes up if I were you. The odds are against it. People go missing, he said. Addicts especially. The street absorbs them. Your friend might be living in a ditch.

He did not say these words with the distancing sarcasm or condescension that straight men sometimes use on queers. He simply sounded bored and hopeless.

Matthew Quinn. First he was Matt. Then he was Matty. These two syllables formed on my tongue as I spoke his name repeatedly into his ear and then into his mouth. That was before he was gone.

This is how we'd met: I had come by the clinic, the one where he worked, to deliver some medical supplies from the company I was then working for, and I saw him near a window whose slatted light fell across the face of a feverish young woman who lay on a bed under mosquito netting. She was resting quietly with her eyes closed and her hand rising to her forehead in an almost unconscious gesture. She was very thin. You could see it in her skinny veined forearms and her prominent cheekbones. On one cheekbone was a J-shaped scar.

Close by, a boy about nine years old sat on a chair watching her. I had the impression that they had both been there, mother and son, for a week or so. Four other patients immobilized by illness were in other beds scattered around the room. Outside a dog barked in the local language, Amharic, and the air inside remained motionless except for some random agitation under a rattling ceiling fan. The hour was just past midday, and very hot.

That's when I noticed Quinn: he was approaching the

woman with a cup in his hand, and after getting himself underneath the mosquito netting, he supported her head as he helped her drink the water, or medicine (I couldn't see what it was), in the cup. Then he turned and, still under the mosquito netting, spoke to the boy in Amharic. His Amharic was better than mine, but I could understand it. He was saying that the boy's mother would be all right but that her recovery would take some time.

The boy nodded.

It was a small, simple gesture of kindness, his remembering to speak to that child. Not everybody would go to the effort. Even when the woman's husband arrived—sweaty, gesticulating, his eyes narrowed with irritation and fear—to complain about the conditions, Quinn smiled, sat him down, and calmed him. Soon the three of them were speaking softly, so that I could not hear what they said.

Young white Americans come to Africa all the time, some to make money, as I did, others in the grip of mostly harmless youthful idealistic delusions. Much of the time, they are operating out of the purest postcolonial sentimentality. I was there on business, for which I don't apologize. But when I saw that this man, Matty Quinn, was indeed doing good works without any hope of reward, it touched me. Compassion was an unthinking habit with him. He was kind by nature, without anyone asking him to be.

Sometimes you arrive at love before going through the first stage of attraction. The light from the window illuminated his body as he helped that sick woman and then squatted down to speak to the boy and his father. After that I found myself imprinted with his face; it gazed at me in daydreams. Here it is, or was: slightly narrow, with hooded eyes and thick eyebrows over modestly stubbled cheeks, and sensual lips from which that day came words of solace so tenderhearted that I thought: *This isn't natural; he must be queer.* And indeed he was, as I found out, sitting with him in a café a week later over cups of the local mudlike coffee. He didn't realize how his kindness and his charity had pierced me until I told him about my own vulnerabilities, and the erotic directions in which I was inclined, whereupon he looked at me with an expression of amused relief. When I confessed how the sight of him had stunned me, he said, very thoughtfully, "I can help you with that," and he put his hand on my knee so quickly that even I hardly noticed the gesture.

Being white and gay in Ethiopia is no easy matter, but we managed it by meeting on weekends in the nearest city. We'd go to multinational hotels, the impersonal expense-account Hiltons with which I am familiar and where they don't care who you are. In those days, before he got sick, Matty Quinn walked around with a lilt, his arm half-raised in a potential greeting, as if he were seeking voters. His good humor and sense made his happiness contagious. A good soul has a certain lightness and lifts up those who surround it. He lifted me. We fucked like champions and then poured wine for each other. I loved him for himself and for how he made me feel. I wonder if Jesus had that effect on people. I think so.

By the time we both came back to the States, however, Quinn was already sick. I said I could fly out to see him, but he asked me not to, given his present condition. He was living in a friend's basement, he told me, and was looking around for a job, and he didn't want me to visit until his circumstances had improved. That was untrue, about the job. Instead, he was losing himself. He was breaking down. He was particulating. When he disappeared, I resolved to find him.

Entering The Lower Depths, the bar on Hennepin that I finally identified as the place Quinn had described to me, I saw, through the tumult of louts near the entryway, a man sitting at the back of the bar, reading a book. He did not have graying black hair, but he did wear glasses, so I made my way toward him, reflexively curling my fingers into fists. I elbowed into a nearby space and ordered a beer. After waiting for a lull in the background noise and finding none, I shouted, "What's that you're reading?"

"Shakespeare!"

"Which play?"

"Not a play! The sonnets."

"Well, I'll be! 'When in disgrace with fortune and men's eyes!' " I quoted loudly, with a calculating, companionable smile on my face. I extended my hand. "Name's Albert. Harry Albert."

The man nodded but did not extend his hand in return. "Two first names? Well, I'm Blackburn."

"Black Bird?"

"No. Blackburn. Horace Blackburn."

"Right. My friend told me about you!"

"Who's your friend?"

"Matt Quinn."

Blackburn shook his head. "Don't know him."

"Okay, you don't know him. But do you know where I might find him?"

"How could I know where he is if I don't know him?"

"Just a suspicion!" Doing business in central Africa, I had gotten used to wily characters; I was accustomed to their smug expressions of guarded cunning. They always gave themselves away by their self-amused trickster smirks. I had learned to keep pressing on these characters until they just got irritated with me.

"Come on, Mr. Blackburn," I said. "Let's not pretend. Let's get in the game here and then go to the moon, all right?"

"I don't know where he is," Blackburn insisted. I wondered how long this clown had carried on as a pseudo-Indian peddling narcotic painkillers to low-life addicts and to upstanding citizens who then became addicts. Probably for years, maybe since childhood. And the Shakespeare! Just a bogus literary affectation. He smelled of breath mints and had a tattoo on his neck.

"However," he said slyly, "if I were looking for him, I'd go down to the river and I'd search for him in the shadows by the Hennepin Avenue Bridge." Blackburn then displayed an unwitting smile. "Guys like that turn into trolls, you know?" His eyes flashed. "Faggot trolls especially."

Reaching across with guarded delicacy, I spilled the man's 7UP over his edition of Shakespeare, dropped some money on the bar, and walked out. If this unregistered barroom brave wanted to follow me, I was ready. Every man should know how to throw a good punch, gay men especially. I have a remarkably quick combination of left jabs and a right uppercut, and I can take a punch without crumpling. Mine is not a glass jaw. You hit me, you hit a stone.

Outside the bar, I asked a policeman to point me in the direction of the Mississippi River, which he did with a bored, hostile stare.

I searched down there that night for Quinn, and the next night I searched for him again. For a week I patrolled the riverbank, watching the barges pass, observing the joggers, and inhaling the pleasantly fetid river air. I kept his face before me as lovers do, a light to guide me, and like any lover I was single-minded. I spoke his name in prayer. Gradually I widened the arc of my survey to include the areas around the university and the hospitals. Many dubious characters presented themselves to me, but I am a fighter and did not fear them.

One night around one a.m., I was walking through one of the darkest sections along the river, shadowed even during the day by canopies of maple trees, when I saw in the deep obscurity a solitary man sitting on a park bench. I could make him out from the pinpoint reflected light from buildings on the other bank. He was barely discernible there, hardly a man at all, he had grown so thin.

Approaching him, I saw that this wreck was my beloved Matty Quinn, or what remained of him. I called his name. He turned his head toward me, and gave me a look of recognition colored over with indifference. He did not rise to greet me, so I could not hug him. He emanated an odor of the river, as if he had been living in it. After I sat down next to him, I tenderly took him into my arms as if he would break. But he had already been broken. I kissed his cheek. Something terrible had happened to him, but he recognized me; he knew me.

"I was afraid it was you, Harry," he said. "I was afraid you would find me."

"Of course I would find you. I went searching."

He lifted up his head as if listening for something. "Do you think we're all being watched? Do you think anything is watching us?" At first I thought he meant surveillance cameras, and then I understood that he was referring to the gods.

"No," I said. "Nothing is ever watching us, Matty. We're all unwatched." Then I said, "I want you to come back with me. I have a hotel room. Let me feed you and clean you up and clothe you. I should never have left you alone, goddamn it. I shouldn't have let you end up back here. Come with me. Look at you. You're shivering."

"This is very sweet of you," he said. "You're admirable. But the thing is, I keep waiting for him." He did not elaborate.

"Who?"

"I keep waiting for that boy. Remember? That mother's boy? And then when he shows up, I always hit him with a baseball bat." This was pure dissociation.

"You're not making any sense," I said. "Let's go. Let's get you in the shower and wash you down and order a big steak from room service."

"No, he's coming," he insisted. "He'll be here any minute,

propelled by thorns." And then, out of nowhere, he said, "I love you, but I'm not here now. And I won't be. Harry, give it up. Let's say goodbye."

I'm a businessman, very goal- and task-oriented, and I won't stand for talk like that. "Come on," I said. "Matty. Enough of this shit. Let's go. Let's get out of here." I stood before him and raised him by his shoulders as if he were a huge rag doll, and together, with my arm supporting him, we walked along the river road until by some miracle a taxi approached us. I hailed it, and the man drove us back to my hotel. In the lobby, the sight we presented—of a successful well-groomed gentleman holding up a shambling, smelly wreck—raised an eyebrow at the check-in desk from the night clerk, but eyebrows have never inflicted a moment of pain on me.

I bathed him that night, and I shaved him, and I ordered a cheeseburger from room service, from which he ate two bites fed from my hand to his mouth. I put him to bed in clean sheets, and all night he jabbered and shivered and cried out and tried to fight me and to escape. He actually thought he could defeat me physically, that's how deluded he was. The next day, after a few phone calls, I checked him in to a rehab facility—they are everywhere in this region, and he was quite willing to go—and I promised to return in ten days for a visit. They don't want you sooner than that.

Matty Quinn was right: he was now a different man, his soul ruined by his dealings with Black Bird, or Blackburn, or whatever that scholar of Shakespeare was calling himself these days, and I did not love him anymore. I felt fairly certain that I had gone through a one-way gate and would not be able to love him again. I can be fickle, I admit. Yet I would not abandon him until he was ready for it. In the meantime, out of the love I had once felt for him, and which it had been my honor to possess, I resolved to kill his enabler.

The next night, I lured Black Bird outside The Lower Depths. I informed him that I had brought with me a bulging packet of cash, and that I would give it to him for the sake of my friend Quinn's painkilling drugs. But the cash was outside, I said, and only I could show him where. I did my best to look like a sucker.

Once in the shadows, I worked quickly and efficiently on him, and then after some minutes I left Black Bird battered on the brick pavement out of sight of the bar's alley entryway. The man was a drug dealer, and I had administered to him the hard professional beating I thought he deserved. I would have beaten Matty's doctor too, the one who first prescribed the painkillers, but they don't let you do that; you can't assault our medical professionals. Black Bird had gotten the brunt of it. But the angel of justice calls for retribution in kind, and since Matty Quinn was still alive, so, in his way, was Black Bird.

When Matty was ready to be discharged, I returned to Minneapolis and picked him up. Imagine this: the sun was blazing, and in broad daylight the man I had once loved folded himself up into my slate-gray rental car, and we drove like any old couple to the basement where he had been staying. We picked up his worldly possessions, the ones he wished to keep and to take with him to Seattle. Remnants: a high school yearbook, photographs of the village where he had worked in Ethiopia, a pair of cuff links, a clock radio, a laptop computer, a few books, and clothes, including a dark blue ascot. Not loving him, I helped him pack, and, not loving him, I bought him a ticket back to Seattle.

Saying very little, we sat together on the plane, touching hands occasionally. Not loving him, I moved him temporarily into my condo, and took him around Seattle and showed him how to use its public transportation system, and located a job for him in a deli. Together we found him a twelve-step program for drug addicts in recovery.

He lives nearby in an apartment I hunted down for him, and we have gone on with our lives. I call him almost every night, whether I am here or away on business.


Slowly, he is taking charge of his life. It seems a shame to say so, but because the light in his soul is diminished, the one in mine, out of sympathy, is diminished too. I cry occasionally, but unsentimentally, and we still take pleasure in bickering, as we always have. His inflammations still cause him pain, and he moves now with small steps like an old man, but when I am in town I bring him dinners from Trader Joe's and magazines from the drugstore, and, one night, he brought home a sandwich for me that he himself had made at the deli. As I bit into the rye bread and corned beef, he watched me. "You like it?" he asked.

"It's fine," I said, shrugging. "Sauerkraut's a bit thick."

"That's how I do it," he said crossly, full of rehab righteousness.

"And I like more Russian dressing than this." I glanced out the window. "Moon's out," I said. "Full, I think. Werewolf weather."

He looked at it. "You never see the moon," he said, "until you sit all night watching it and you see how blindly stupid and oafish it is. I used to talk to it. My whole autobiography. Looked like the same moon I saw in Africa, but it wasn't. Never said a damn word in return once I was here. Over there, it wouldn't shut up."

"Well, it doesn't have anything to say to Americans," I remarked, my mouth full. "We're beyond that. Anything on TV?"

"Yeah," he said, "junkie TV, where people are about to die from their failings. Then they're rescued by Dr. Phil and put on the boat to that enchanted island they have." He waited. I got the feeling that he didn't believe in his own recovery. Or in the American project. Maybe we weren't really out of the woods.

"Okay, here's what I want you to do," he said. "I want you to call up this Benjamin Takemitsu person and tell him that I owe him some money." He laughed at the joke. Even his eyes lit up at the prankster aspect of making amends and its bourgeois comforts. "Tell him I'll pay him eventually. I'll pay him ten cents on the dollar."

"That's a good one."

"Hey, even Plato was disappointed by the material world. Me too."

"Gotcha."

"Pour me a drink," he commanded. I thought I knew what he was going to do, so I gave him what he wanted, some Scotch with ice, despite my misgivings.

"Here's how you do it," he said, when he had the Scotch in his hand. "Remember what they did in Ethiopia, that ceremonial thing?" He slowly upended the drink and emptied it out on my floor, where it puddled on the dining room tile. "In memory of those who are gone. In memory of those down below us."

It felt like a toast to our former selves. You're supposed to do it outside, on the ground, not in a building, but I followed along, inverting my beer bottle. The beer gurgled out onto the dining room floor, and I smiled as if something true and actual had happened, this imported ritual, imagining that he would probably be all right after all. Quinn smiled back, triumphant.

# Forbearance

Whenever Amelia gazed at the olive trees outside, she could momentarily distract herself from the murderous poetry on the page in front of her.

*Esto lavá çaso, metlichose çantolet íbsefelt sed syrt*
*Int çantolet ya élosete stnyt en, alardóowet arenti myrt.*

Getting these lines into English was like trying to paint the sun blue. In several years as a translator, she'd never found another text so unmanageable. The poem was titled "Impossibility," and that's what it was. Each time she looked at the words, she felt as if she were having a stroke; she could feel her face getting numb and sagging on one side. Meanwhile, the ironic ticking of the wall clock marked the unproductive seconds as they shuffled past. The clock loved its job, even though the time it told was wildly inaccurate. The owner of this villa, a charming old Italian woman, had informed Amelia that the clock was senile and delusional like everyone else in the village and must never be adjusted. Adjusting it would hurt its feelings.

"That clock thinks it's on Mars," the old woman had told Amelia in a conspiratorial whisper. "It tells you what time it is there. And *you*, an American, want to argue with it?"

The poem in front of Amelia on the desk had been written

near the beginning of the nineteenth century, in an obscure Botho-Ugaric dialect combining the language of courtly love with warfare, with an additional admixture of *liebestod,* called *mordmutt* in this dialect. The idioms of love and war should have blended together but didn't. In some not-so-subtle manner, the poet seemed to be threatening his beloved with mayhem if she refused to knuckle under to him. The language of these threats (*Int çantolet ya élosete,* for example: "I could murder you with longing," or, more accurately, "My longing longs to murder"), inflated with metaphors and similes of baroque complication, was as gorgeous as an operatic aria sung by a charming baritone addressing a woman who was being flung around onstage and who wasn't allowed to open her mouth. *And it was all untranslatable!* You couldn't heat up soggy English verbs and nouns to a boil the way you could in this dialect, which actually had a word for love bites, *muttzemp.*

Amelia put down her pen and tapped her fingers. The decorative clock, painted green, was amused by her troubles. *There's* a second of your life you'll never get back! And *there:* there's another one! Too bad you're not on Mars like me. There's lots of time on Mars. We've got nothing but time here! Today is like yesterday! Always was!

With a tiny advance from a publisher and a six-week deadline, she felt like a caged animal hopping on electrified grates for the occasional food pellet. Her professional reputation was at stake: after this volume was published, she would probably be held up to ridicule in *The New York Review of Books* for her translation of this very poem. She could already see the adverb-adjective clusters: "discouragingly inept," "sadly inappropriate," "amusingly tin-eared." One of the few Americans who had any command of this dialect, she belonged to a tight little society full of backbiters. The other poems hadn't been terribly hard to translate, but so far this one had defeated her. *Let me murder you,* the poet demanded, *and we'll descend to the depths together / where darkness enfolds us in*—what?—*the richest watery silks. / Down, down, to the obscurest nethermost regions, / where sea creatures writhe in amorous clutchings . . .*

Awful. The olive trees didn't care what she was doing, so she looked at them gratefully. Downstairs, her twenty-year-old son and his girlfriend were making love-noises. Chirps. Impossible! Everything was impossible.

This particular afternoon, in the little Tuscan villa she had rented a month ago, Jack, her son, and Gwyneth, the girlfriend, were cooking up sausage lasagna. They cooed at each other after coaxing the pan into the oven. Over the noise of the clock, Amelia listened to their endearments. Here she was, enjoying the voyeurism of the middle-aged parent. After several minutes, she could hear them washing the ingredients for salad, speaking lovely birdsong Italian to each other. Through the years, Jack had spent so much time over here in boarding school that his Italian was better than his mother's. He didn't even have the trace of an American accent that Amelia had. Gwyneth, like Jack, was bilingual (her father was English and had married a local Italian), but she and Jack preferred Italian for their intimacies, as who would not?

The hour: too early for preparing dinner! What did those two scamps think they were up to? Gwyneth, beautiful and bossy in the Italian manner, though she was a blonde, held

Amelia's lovesick son tightly in her grip; she gave orders to him followed by gropes and love-rewards. They had met a mere three weeks ago. Love happened fast in this region, like a door slammed open. Amelia had seen those two trying to prepare dishes together while holding hands. Very touching, but comical.

She glanced at her watch: actually, the day was almost over, and the day's work was kaput, obliterated. She had struggled all afternoon on those stupidly impossible poetic lines full of masculine posturing, and now she had nothing. She felt word-nausea coming on.

The poet she was translating fancied himself a warrior type—aristocratic, arrogant, and proud. In one tiny corner of the world, mentioning his name—Imyar Sorovinct—would open doors and get you a free meal. But elsewhere, here in Italy and in the States, he was mostly unknown, except for the often-anthologized "I Give It All Up," his uncharacteristically detached and Zen-like deathbed poem. In midlife he'd presented himself in verse as a man supremely confident of his weapons, arrogantly imploring his beloved to join him in what he called "The Long Night." The particular line on which she had spent the last two hours contained consonant clusters that sounded like distant nocturnal battlefield explosions.

In real life, however, Sorovinct hadn't been a military man at all but a humble tailor of army uniforms, a maker of costumes, driven to poetic fantasies about the men who inhabited them. Bent over, he cut and stitched, ruining his eyesight in the bad light. To no one's surprise, then or now, the poet had been unhappily married. Together, he and his wife had

had a child who, as they said in those days, "never grew up." Cognitively, the son remained a child for all of his twenty-three years before his death, by drowning.

*Armored for sorrow, steeling my resolve, I sing/cry/proclaim (to) you our love-glue*

In English, the vulgarity was shockingly nonsensical, and it missed the force of the verb in the original and suggested nothing of the poet's menace. "Love-glue"! *Muttplitz* in the dialect. What Walt Whitman meant when he used the word "adhesiveness." No real English word existed for it, thank God.

Downstairs, a cork came out of a wine bottle.

They were going to fall into bed and make love any minute now, those two kids. At least someone was having a good time. No point whatever in trying to stop them, unless Amelia could appeal to Gwyneth's probably nonexistent Catholic morality. Should she mention the necessity of contraception? They'd just laugh. She came downstairs to see them pouring two glasses of the cheap blood-dark Chianti you could buy for almost nothing in this region. Just as if she weren't standing there, they raised the glasses to each other's lips.

Gwyneth's hard little face, bravely glassy-eyed, turned toward Amelia, and she smiled in the way that young people do when they know they've been dealt a good hand.

"Going out, darlings," Amelia said. "Just for a minute. Have to buy cigarettes. Be back soon."

"Well, don't be long," Gwyneth commanded with her charming Brit-Euro accent, putting the wineglass down on the counter and raising her finger in a comic admonitory fashion. "Food'll get cold. Hurry back." She leaned away from Jack for a moment so that he could admire her bella figura.

Jack, handsome in his khakis and soft blue shirt, turned toward his mother.

"Momma," he said, "what's this about cigarettes? You don't *smoke.*"

"Well, guess what? It's a perfectly good time to start." She tried to straighten her hair, which probably looked witchy after so much futile desk work. "After a day like this one, I need a new affectation. I need to be *bad*. I need to be bad right now. If they're selling cigarettes, I'm buying them."

"Then you better buy a lighter and an ashtray too," her son reminded her.


She had leased an old Fiat from a man the villagers claimed was a part-time burglar. It was probably a stolen car. After starting the engine, she turned on the radio, hoping to hear Donizetti or Bellini, or at least *somebody*. Instead, they were playing Cher's "If I Could Turn Back Time," a mean-spirited irony considering how the day had gone. The gods laughed easily in the late afternoon, watching human futility fold up for the day. All poetry, good or bad, made the gods laugh. To the gods, poems were sour useless editorials, like bitchy letters to Santa. The Fiat coughed and hesitated as Amelia first passed by a vineyard, then, on the other side of the road, a painterly haystack. One old bespectacled man, holding a walking stick, ambled along the road, going in the opposite direction. He doffed his cap at her, and she waved at him. A single blue-flecked bird, chirping in Italian, flew overhead.

But nature was unforgiving. The sun, lowering toward the west, recited one of the lines that Amelia couldn't translate: *Féyitçate fyr tristo, eertch tye mne muttplitz.*

By the time she reached the village, after negotiating three hairpin turns and avoiding death by collision from an errant truck out of whose way she had swerved in a last-minute effort to save her own life, she could feel the sweat in her palms oozing out onto the steering wheel. No water came from the fountain in the town square: the pump had been broken for weeks, and there was no money to fix it. The air smelled of burnt rope. A brownish liquid flowed in the gutter. She parked her car, turned off the ignition, and waited until the motor coughed and sputtered and dieseled its way into silence. An American couple sitting in the square's sidewalk café gazed at her with tourist-interest, as if she were a quaint item of local color. Amelia hurried into the general store, where she was greeted by the owner, Signor Travatini, a timid man who had a tendency to avoid her gaze; he was probably in love with her, or maybe he was planning on hiring someone to rob her.

"My dear Carlo," she said. "How are you? It's been a terrible day." Italian, with its languorous vowels, was sheer pleasure after a day's struggle with the Botho-Ugaric dialect.

"Yes," he said, looking out toward the village square and her car. "Yes, and the sun has passed its way through the sky once again. Things are not translating? Sometimes they do not. Sometimes they stubbornly stay what they are. I am sorry."

"No. Things are not translating. I need some cigarettes," she said.

"Ah, but you do not smoke." Everyone here kept track of everyone else's habits, and the villagers all knew her by now.

"After such a day as I have had, I think it would be a good time to learn."

He shrugged. "You are correct. As we get old, we need to acquire new vices. God will not be interested in us otherwise. We must wave our arms at Him to get His attention. It is the end of the day, so I will speak to you in confidence. I myself have attracted God's attention by acquiring a new . . . how do you say this in English? *Ragazza.*"

"Girlfriend."

"Yes. I have acquired a new *girlfriend*. Perhaps I am being too bold in saying so." He stared at the cash register, harmlessly confabulating. The man was in his midfifties, and his pudgy wife, Claudia, dressed in black, sometimes lumbered into the store to do the accounts, and was known everywhere in the village for her terrible tongue lashings. Like Imyar Sorovinct, Carlo Travatini had earned a right to his fantasies. "My *girlfriend* loves me. And of course I adore her. She tells me that she admires my patience and my skill at lovemaking, despite my advanced years. The years give us older men a certain . . . technical skill. Forgive me for being so crude." Amelia shook her head, disclaiming any possible shock. "Why do I tell you this? I do so because our love, hers and mine, is an open secret. I will not, however, give you the young lady's name, because I should not wish to appear to be indiscreet. We Italians are not noted for our subtlety or discretion. We are announcers and are combustible. We announce first this, then that. In this announcing manner I have written poems for her, my *beloved*. Would you like to see my poems? They are of course not at the level of Montale, but . . ." He began to fumble in his pocket. Amelia stopped him in the midst of his harmless comic charade.

"No, thank you." More love poems! They came out of the woodwork everywhere and should be outlawed. There was far too much love, a worldwide glut of it. *What the world needs now,* she thought, *is much less love.* "How wonderful for you. But, please, no."

"All right. But I beg of you, do not mention the beautiful young woman to my wife, in case you should see her."

"I shall say nothing," Amelia told him. "What cigarettes do you have? I would like an Italian brand."

"Well, we have Marlboros. Sturdy cigarettes in a crush-proof box. And L & M. That is a good brand also."

"Both American. No, I want an Italian cigarette."

"Well, let me see. I have MS."

"MS?" She felt a moment of pity.

"Yes. MS. Of course. It is a brand of cigarette we have here. Monopoli di Stato. You should know that by now. Filtro? Or Blu?"

"Blu, please." He brought down a pack on which appeared, in rather large letters, the Italian phrase for "Smoking kills."

"You should not do this," he said, putting the cigarette pack into her hand with a tender gesture, brushing her fingers as he did so. "It is no way to get God's attention. You should get a *boy*friend, perhaps?"

"Also, I need some matches, please."

He reached under the counter and brought some out. He shook his head as she paid him for the cigarettes. "After all these years," he said, "I do not understand you Americans.

Forgive me. I have been listening to the news on the radio just now. Iraq, Afghanistan. You are unexplainable, indefinable. So friendly and yet so warlike. This contradiction . . . I cannot understand it."

"Yes," Amelia said. "You are right. We are puzzling and incomprehensible. Thank you, my friend. Ciao."

"Ciao, signora," he said, looking away from her again, down at his hands. "Grazie." What a sorrowful man, she thought, with his sorrow painstakingly narrated every day. You would never see such a man in the States. She had almost returned to the stolen Fiat when her Italian cell phone rang. When she answered, there was silence. She hung up.

The American couple waved her over. They were drinking wine.

"Hey there. Good afternoon," the man said in English with a slight southwestern accent. "Care to join us?" He wore a Tyrolean hat, a blue shirt, a tan-colored sport coat, a string tie, and cowboy boots. His wife, deeply tanned, wearing a plain gray dress and a collection of thin gold bracelets that rattled like jail keys, smiled nervously upward at the sky, avoiding eye contact. She had very expensive hair, Amelia noted, highlighted with blond streaks.

"How did you know I was an American?" Amelia asked.

"Aw, you look like one of us," the man told her. "It's a duck recognizing another duck." The wife nodded at the sky. Amelia felt all her strength leaving her body: she was heavily invested in appearing to be Italian or French, with a trace of beautiful haughtiness, or at least generically European snobbishness, and if she could be exposed this easily by lunkheads, then her nationality might indeed be an essence that no role-playing could disguise. Being an American was a curse—you were so recognizable everywhere that your nationality was like a clown suit. Maybe Jack would escape it. She had come to think of her own countrymen as *them*. She shivered. After all her efforts, she was instantly identifiable and still looked like one of *them*. Fucking hell.

"Sorry," she said. "I have to get back. They've prepared lasagna," she said. "The kids."

"We're going to be here in town for a few days," the man said, before gulping down half his glass of wine. "You just drop in on us any old time. We got ourselves that villa up the hill. There for the whole week."

"Okay," she said, before waving goodbye to them.


On one of the hairpin turns on the way back, her phone rang again, and this time, when she answered it, the voice that came out—the connection was poor—sounded like her brother.

"Amelia?"

"Yes?" She held the cell phone in her left hand as she downshifted with her right. The steering wheel wobbled. "Jerry? Is that you, Jerry?"

"Yeah. Of course it's Jerry. Who'd you think it was?" Amelia let her foot off the clutch, and the car lurched into the lower gear. "Sorry. That was rude. I'm really sorry. I mean, we're on pins and needles here. I'm a damn mess, is what it is. Yvonne's a mess, too."

"What is it? What's going on?" There was another pause for the transatlantic long distance or for her brother's hesitation. "Is it Catherine?"

"Yes, of course it's Catherine. She's taken a bad turn. The doctors have been saying that . . . actually, I don't really know *what* they've been saying. It's all a jumble to me. But like I say, she's worse. Now her kidneys aren't working. And that's on top of everything else. The pneumonia. But I'm not saying you should come here. I'm not saying that."

"Of course I'll come," Amelia said to her brother. "I'll be there as soon as possible."

"Thanks," he said. "We could use some bucking up." Amelia heard another voice in the background, and then her brother said goodbye and broke off the connection.

As soon as she had parked close to the villa, she emptied herself out of the car, looked at the package of cigarettes in her hand, and went inside. The table had been set, and Gwyneth and Jack were waiting for her on the sofa, both of them beautiful and radiant. This world was paradise, after all, when your son and his girlfriend, healthy and in love with each other, cooked dinner for you inside a cool dark Italian villa, and you could worry all day about a line of poetry that you couldn't translate properly, and you could be annoyed by simpleton American tourists. To be bothered by trivialities was sheer heaven.

"Momma," Jack said. "What happened to you?"

"Your cousin Catherine's worse," Amelia said, tossing the cigarettes onto a side table, as if she'd never bought them. "I'm going to have to fly to Minneapolis. You two will have to hold down the fort here for a few days. Can you do that? I'll even leave you the Fiat if you drive me to the airport."

Jack nodded. Gwyneth rose and walked over to Amelia, taking her hand as if she were offering preliminary condolences. "Do you still want dinner?" she asked. The girl gave off a musky odor, and her face was slightly flushed and sleepy; naturally they'd had quick sex in Amelia's absence, and now they'd be soft and cuddly and compliant.

"Of course," Amelia said. "Of course, of course. And let's get drunk. Okay? Are you willing to do that?"

They all laughed. Laughing, Jack asked, "So what's Catherine worse with?"

"She's dying," Amelia said. "She can't breathe. That's what she's worse with."

Although she loved him, of course, Amelia didn't like her brother very much, mostly because of his employment situation. He worked for a Minneapolis real estate tycoon, Ben Schneiderman, a feral-looking man barely over five feet tall, whose customary expression—Amelia had met him once— was one of superpredatory avarice that mingled from time to time with his one other singular expression, massive sleepy indifference whenever matters of common human experience, those that were not for sale, were exposed to him. Schneiderman had run several newspapers into the ground, bought and sold a few major league teams, and built multiple granite-and-glass high-rises and shopping malls. His wife, Bitsy Christianson, was a patron of the arts. Their personal website (and editorial sounding board) was www.whatsittoyou.com. They owned eight or nine homes. Schneiderman had said many times that his motto was *I never suffer. And neither should you.* Jerry served as the primary consigliere for Schneiderman's various enterprises and spent much of his life on a private jet, scurrying from one financial brush fire to another. He negotiated, threatened, and placated. Amelia's brother was balding from all the stress and had taken to brushing his remaining hair, like tendrils or waterweeds, across the top of his scalp.

And of course there was the other thing: Jerry supported his sister financially. Some of Schneiderman's money trickled down to her. He had paid for Jack's private schools in Switzerland and Italy. Her brother's charity was Amelia's safety net, along with alimony from Jack's father, the man who had caused Amelia to swear off love forever. Well, no one's hands were clean.

But now, in the St. Mary's Hospital's ICU, while Yvonne sat next to the bed holding her daughter's hand, Jerry leaned back against the window, and the blank stare on his face showed Amelia exactly how inwardly broken her brother actually was. She went up to him and hugged him and pecked him on the cheek and quickly did the same to Yvonne, whose cheeks were tear-streaked. In the bed, her niece seemed to be gasping for breath. Another man was in the room, introduced to Amelia as the child's pediatrician, Dr. Elijah Jones, who wore rainbow suspenders with cartoon faces on them. Everybody thanked Amelia for coming.

"Anyone would have done it," she said. "You would have done it for me, if Jack, God forbid, got sick. Where's Gerald?" Gerald was Catherine's little brother.

"He's home with the babysitter," Jerry said, with a sigh. "The poor kid. We've been neglecting him. Can't be helped."

The pediatrician, after a few pleasantries, took Amelia down the hall and told her that her brother needed as much comfort and solace as she could give him, and that it was a good thing she was there. He pulled off his glasses and cleaned the lenses with his Donald Duck necktie. He explained about the gradual impairment of Catherine's muscular control. Amelia nodded. "You have to try to love everybody," the doctor said, embarrassed but also in earnest, as he smiled sadly. "They all need it. All of them." When Amelia asked about the prognosis, the doctor shrugged. "Your brother and sister-in-law have been holding on. They're the ones I'm worried about. Your niece . . . well, we're doing everything we can."

She left the hospital with her heart pounding. She had always desperately loved pediatricians.

So bleary with jet lag that she could not sleep or make any sense in conversation, and feeling that her brain was a haunted house in which bats flew randomly from one attic beam to another, Amelia found herself at two a.m. walking outside her hotel and then along the Mississippi River. Catherine had been a beautiful baby but had been sickly, and, like Sorovinct's son, she had multiple afflictions that had prevented her from growing into adolescence. She had remained a child for her entire life. One time when Amelia had been visiting, Catherine had approached her with a calendar she'd made herself with a ruler and crayons. Two pages: the months of April and May. Her niece had listed a price for the calendar at the top: fifty cents for each page. Amelia had bought the two calendar months and taken them home and put them up on the refrigerator, only to discover that they were inaccurate and in some sense imaginary. Her niece had filled in the date boxes any way she wanted to. They were surrealist calendars, with dates that would never exist: Tuesday, May 14, 2011, for example. Wednesday, May 15. There would never be such days.

Amelia had loved Catherine. Why should such a child suffer? Or any child? Sitting on a bench that looked out at the Stone Arch Bridge, Amelia thought of Ivan Karamazov speaking of the suffering of children and saying, "I don't understand anything, and I don't *want* to understand anything," and as the river flowed past her on its journey to the Gulf of Mexico, she leaned forward and put her head in her hands before straightening up again to wipe her face free of the tears that had accumulated there. Lucky me with my son, Jack; lucky Jack with his girlfriend; lucky me, she thought, and if I could only share my luck with everybody, every living soul, I would.

She walked back to her hotel, trudged up to her room, undressed again, and put on her nightgown. Maybe this time she'd find a hour or two of sleep. Almost as soon as her head touched the pillow, she entered a dream of astounding specificity: she was sitting in a slightly dingy living room in Eastern Europe, lit with four candles in pewter candleholders. To her left was a small sturdy wooden dinner table set for two, and in front of her was a fireplace in which the coals appeared to be dying. The room had a smoky and unclean smell. A mongrel dog sat to her right and barked once at her, as if the dream could now commence. It was like a film director shouting, "Action!" Amelia knew, without knowing how she knew, that she had found herself in Imyar Sorovinct's home and that the poet's wife stood off to the side, just out of sight, preparing a meal. In front of her, sitting in another chair, was Imyar Sorovinct.

The poet held himself up with straight soldierly posture, like a veteran in a wheelchair, but his face betrayed him: his left eye, lower than his right, looked at Amelia with patient compassion, while his right eye gazed on indifferently, as if two separate selves were housed within him. His uncombed hair rose wildly from the back of his scalp, and his large ears stuck out from his head like jug handles. He was a very homely man with no appealing features. His hands trembled as they rested on his thighs. The expression on Sorovinct's face was one of scrupulous interest dimmed by time-distance and dream-distance, both of which were causing him to disintegrate.

Amelia waited for him to speak. When he said nothing, she told him, in his native dialect, "My name is Amelia, and I . . ."

"I know who you are," Sorovinct told her in perfect English. "You've been trying to translate 'Impossibility.'"

"You do? Well. Then you know that I can't get anywhere with that poem."

"And you never will," Sorovinct told her. "You'll never get that one right. You'll just have to give it up."

"I hate to. I've spent so long on it."

"Too bad," Sorovinct said, rubbing his chin. "Just forget it." He picked up his book of poems from the floor and opened it in front of her. "There's something I want you to do," he said. He pointed at a page, where a poem entitled "Forbearance" appeared. "This is the poem you should be translating. It's more compatible with you. And the tone? Much easier. You'll manage this one in no time, believe me. Please just do what I ask. Also, and I don't mean to be rude, but it would be better if you did it right now."

The dog to Amelia's right barked twice, as if saying, "Cut! Print!"

She awoke and turned on the bedside light. It was four a.m. She went over to her suitcase, took out the volume of Sorovinct's poetry, and turned to the poem he had pointed to. After sitting down at the hotel room desk, she reached for her pen and translated the poem line by line, each line almost instantly suggesting its equivalent in English. She wrote out the translation on the hotel's stationery. The entire process took less than thirty minutes. The poem didn't really sound Sorovinct's characteristic note, but so what? She was under orders. When she returned to bed, the time was five minutes past five o'clock.

She had never seen a dog in a dream before. And the dream hadn't allowed her to say goodbye. Why was that?

At Catherine's memorial service, midway through, Amelia rose to speak, with the hotel stationery in her hand. Looking out at her family, she said, "I want to read a poem by Imyar Sorovinct. I've just translated it. It's called 'Forbearance.' I'm reading it in memory of Catherine." She lowered her head to recite, her voice trembling. "Forbearance," she began.

*Who is the child who stands beside this sea, wind-broken,*
*   wracked*
*With spray that seems to paint his skin with heaven's tears?*
*And who might be this man but the father of the boy,*
*   standing there*
*In wrinkled clothes, holding a halo above the child to keep*
*   him dry*
*Out of sorrow, out of love, at this abrupt and stony seashore*
*Visited in autumnal days? This is the child who clutches at*
*   his father*
*Who intercedes for him, this quiet, vested man guarding*
*   the boy*
*From rain and spray. This is the child who does not speak,*
*Who never speaks, who must be blessed. The gulls are*
*   circling.*
*There is something patient in the waves that they both*
*   imitate,*
*And it is in the rain and spray that one feels the power*
*Of forbearance, in this autumnal drizzle*
*Soaking the parent and his child, loving what is damaged*
*And wholly theirs, held like a precious jewel*
*Tightly, tightly, in their hands together.*

At the cemetery, in broad daylight, when it was her turn, she stabbed the shovel that had been handed to her into the pile of dirt, and, forcing the blade downward, scooped out a measure of clay and sand and soil. She carried the shovelful to the grave site and dropped it over Catherine's casket, on whose surface it made a hollow sound—like a groan from another world, mixed with the sound of her own grief. Then she seemed to wake up and heard the sounds of the others assembled there, and someone took her hand, and someone else took the shovel.

Twenty-four months later, Amelia found herself in Baltimore, sitting in a hotel lobby at a conference of translators. From the cocktail lounge came peals of alcoholic laughter, followed by jokes told in Polish, Russian, French. It was a habit of translators to speak in collage-expressions in which three or four languages were mixed together. Ostentatious drunken polyglots! As she waited for her friend to meet her—they had reservations at Baltimore's best seafood restaurant—she spied, across the lobby, Robert McGonigal, whom she thought of as the Old Translator. He sat slumped there in an ill-fitting suit, focused on the distance, rubbing his forehead above his massively overgrown eyebrows. He wore the thickest eyeglasses Amelia had ever seen, with lenses that made his eyes seem tiny. McGonigal's versions of the *Iliad,* the *Odyssey,* and the *Aeneid* were still being taught in colleges and universities everywhere, as were his translations of Pasternak, whom he had known personally. He had known everybody. But now he was sitting in a hotel lobby alone, wearing a facial expression that said, "I have seen it. You cannot surprise me."

She rose and walked over to where he was sitting. She wanted a blessing from the old man. Jack and Gwyneth were to be married in two months, in Italy. What would the future bring them? There had to be a blessing. McGonigal seemed to be gazing through space-time. Standing in front of him, Amelia introduced herself, and McGonigal nodded at her, as if she were a speck on eternity's wall. Nervously she prattled on, and, as she heard more polyglot joking from the bar, she thought, *Well, I might as well tell him.* Somewhat against her better judgment, she related the story of her efforts to translate Sorovinct's poem "Impossibility."

"I couldn't do it," she said, and McGonigal gave an imperceptible nod. "It just wouldn't go. And then I went to bed, and Sorovinct appeared to me in a dream." McGonigal, startled, suddenly began to look at her closely. "I was in his house," she said. "His wife and dog were there too."

"What happened then?" McGonigal asked, his voice ancient and whispery.

"Well, he told me that I'd never get that poem right. He brought out his book of poems and pointed at another poem."

McGonigal's face took on an air of astonishment.

"And he said, 'This is the poem you must translate. This one you'll get in no time.'"

"So?"

"So I woke up," Amelia said, "and I translated the poem in half an hour."

"I am astonished," McGonigal said, struggling to get to his feet.

"Well, I . . ."

"I am astonished," McGonigal repeated. By now he was standing in front of her unsteadily, studying her carefully. He had taken Amelia's hand. "Are you seriously telling me . . ."

He seemed momentarily incapable of speech. "Are you seriously telling me that that's the *first time* that such a thing has ever happened to you?"

"Well, yes."

"My dear," he said, his voice coming out of eternity. "Oh, my dear." He opened his mouth and exhaled, and his breath smelled of Catherine's grave, and then, as Amelia drew back, the grave started to laugh at her.

PART TWO

# Lust

"Sir," the security guy says, "please move away from the gaming table while you are on the phone." Benny finishes his call to his friend Dennis, who has been giving Benny advice, and he slips his phone into his pocket.

The guard, dressed in a tight sport coat, nods affably, an action that does not seem to come easily to him. He looks like a college-educated brute. He has a crew cut, a Bluetooth in his ear, and a thick neck that tests the collar button on his white shirt. Like those of every other mean motherfucker Benny has ever known, the guard's eyes are as blank as the lens of a camera.

Benny returns to the blackjack table in the Gray Wolf Casino outside the town of Phelps Lake, Minnesota, where he has been trying to lose all the money he has in the world and to mess up his life in a thoroughly convincing way. He's acting out, and he knows it, and his friend Dennis, over the phone, has been telling him so. Nevertheless, he's not succeeding. Two guys seated at the blackjack table have observed Benny with polite disbelief. He had been hoping for a spell of bad luck, but all he can do is win.

Quoting from *Touch of Evil*, he texted Dennis a few hours ago to say that his future was all used up, but he was winning at blackjack nevertheless. Dennis called him right back.

"What's this about your future being all used up?" he asked. "That's from *Touch of Evil*."

"Well, she left me, didn't she?"

"You are in the grip of romantic mindlessness," Dennis told him. "I like that." The man has earned the right to say such things to him. After all, he's attached to a morphine drip and is lying in a hospital bed. "Go on playing if you're winning, Sport," Dennis advised, between coughs. "Never buck a winning streak." Dennis, who is Benny's age, likes to make pronouncements. They're part of his impeccable style.

"I'm roadkill," Benny said.

"No. You're just aggrieved." Dennis coughed again. "Don't forget: the best part of breaking up with a girl and finding a new girl is that all your stories are fresh again."

Black crows of the spirit have been pecking at Benny for eighteen hours—his imagination is inflamed with metaphors, and the metaphors themselves are vampires, sucking the blood from his veins. His girlfriend, Nan, the former love of his life, a tall black-haired beauty in her first year of law school, good-hearted but fickle, broke up with him last night, having traded in Benny for a fellow law student, a triathlete. Nan, too, is a triathlete. "The stars aligned," she told Benny with faux sadness that masked her glee. "His stars and my stars."

Despair seized hold of Benny. Who fights the stars?

The previous night, Benny could see that Nan was doing her best to be diplomatic and kind, a misguided charity that made everything worse. She said, almost in sorrow, that this brand-new fellow with a body she couldn't quite get over was her fate, her *destiny*. What sealed the deal—Nan's phrase—was that the new guy is wildly compassionate and wants to practice what she calls "poverty law" once he passes the bar, making him a shining-armor knight riding to the rescue of the creepazoidal unwashed. Whereas Benny, as a boyfriend, constituted something else: a little oasis where her caravan had briefly stopped, one of those nice-guy interludes for which she would always be grateful.

"I just never fell in love with your niceness," Nan said. "I tried. I guess I couldn't. You're not to blame—you're a great guy, a model citizen. This is all my fault. I'm impaired."

Sitting in a downtown Minneapolis bar with large plate-glass windows, over drinks, she had announced her breakup intentions and in a moment of possibly indeliberate cruelty had held up an iPhone photograph of the shining-armor knight triathlete in question. She displayed her phone full-frontally with the screen facing Benny. Benny ignored it, and he ignored her unsettled facial expression as she said, "There he is. That's him. He's crossing the finish line. Really, can you blame me?"

No one stages a scene in front of plate glass during happy hour, and Benny did not. He sat listening with studied impassivity and noted glumly that Nan had prettied herself for this confrontation—blouse with plunge, heels, necklace, red nail polish—in case of a scene. She'd want to make a good impression on witnesses if there was a first-ever Benny-ish outburst. Her lacquered beauty enraged him, so he sat quietly seething, radiating bogus serenity.

"You're not looking at the picture," Nan said. "I *said* I was sorry about all this."

"Exactly right. I accept your apology."

"Please don't shout."

"You *wish* I were shouting," Benny said, ostentatiously

whispering. "You can hardly hear me. My dial is turned all the way down. We're in the negative numbers now." His hand shaking, Benny took a sip of his festive Bloody Mary. "So what's this guy's name?"

Nan peevishly put her phone back into her purse. "What? His name?"

"Yeah. You know, his *name*."

"Well, his name isn't *him*. A name is so . . . whatever. His identity is his own," Nan said in a vague monotone, watching a toddler walk by outside clutching a teddy bear in one hand, his other hand in his father's. "Okay," she said, apparently gathering her thoughts while rubbing her left knuckle with her right thumb. "So maybe I'll tell you." Clearly the name constituted a difficulty, a distraction. Benny waited for whatever she would say, and while he waited he noticed that she gave off a scent of lavender, which, he feared, was from massage oil.

"Go right ahead," Benny said, sensing an advantage.

"Okay, but you're going to laugh. I *know* you. His name's Thor."

"*Thor?*" Benny exclaimed. "That's a good one. He must be from around here. That's a real Minnesota name for you. Is he a Lutheran?"

"See, I *knew* you would be like that. Under your nice hides the snide. And I have to point out that you're being defensive. Talk about the predictability factor! Like I said, I feel bad for you and I blame myself, but I'm glad I'm moving on to those green pastures they all tell you about."

On the other side of the plate-glass window, civilians went about their business, seemingly indifferent to the wars of love, and from time to time they glanced in at Benny and Nan, the pleasant-looking young couple sitting at a bar table, apparently lost in conversation. The midsummer sun eased itself behind an office building, casting a conical shadow that pierced Benny with melancholy, while the bar slowly filled up with professional-managerial types getting off work in time for happy hour, the men loosening their collars, the women quickly, almost surreptitiously, checking their faces in the mahogany-framed mirror above the bar. To the side, a couple of outcast full-figured ladies in slimming dresses leaned toward each other in the corner, whispering.

The stars wheeled in the empty space of Benny's desolation. He would tell Dennis about the wheeling stars. Dennis would be amused.

He took another sip of his drink as he fought off soul-nausea and the urge to beg. The in-surge of employees getting off work was tidal now. They were making a racket. He would not tell Nan how much he had loved her, the size and mature intensity of that love, its ability to give his life meaning. A man does not beg to be taken back, he reminded himself. Begging qualifies as *the* primary criterion for admission to loserdom, that territory inhabited by platoons of nice vanilla guys who belong in civilized places like Denmark and Sweden, not here in the United States, where they are held in contempt and trampled.

He habitually carries images around in his head. Chained to his consciousness at that moment as he sat across from her was one of Nan. The morning after their first night together, she had stood over his little apartment's gas stove scrambling some eggs for them both, the sunlight streaming through the east window backlighting her hair in glory. She wore a cream-colored nightgown that set off her tanned skin to good effect. Benny and Nan had shared a nearly sleepless night of lovemaking. By morning they were love gods. He rose out of bed with the succulent sea urchin taste of her clitoris still on his tongue. Inspired by the sunlight and her bare feet on the linoleum and her expression of sleepy sensual concentration and the smell of the garlic and the salsa in the eggs, he thought he was the luckiest man alive at that particular hour, that morning, on the planet. Wilhelm Reich was correct: orgasms constituted the meaning of life. The kindly knife of sentiment stabbed at him again and again.

It occurred to him that maybe he hadn't actually known Nan as a person, despite his memories of her. She had said, several times, jokingly, that he was self-deluded. Perhaps she was inexplicable, or maybe he was. Returning to the present moment from his reverie, he tried to look at her across the bar table. Her inexplicable mouth was moving in a half smile: she was saying inexplicable things about how she had felt *that* way then and felt *this* way now. More apologies came out of her.

Following the nausea and the stabbing and the pecking crows and the murderous rage, sadness dropped over him like a cone, inside of which all the oxygen consisted of more sadness. Time undoubtedly passed at Whiskey Sour's, and the waitress replaced his drink with another. Had he said anything? He couldn't remember if he had spoken up or had remained silent as the bar filled with merrymakers, and Nan continued to explain whatever she was explaining. His Bloody Mary glass somehow emptied the Bloody Mary into his mouth. The celery stick in the drink poked at his lip. His mind raced and stopped, raced and stopped. Nan—composed, elegant—sipped her Tom Collins and dabbed her bread in olive oil as she spoke. *What was she saying now?* One woman over at the bar suddenly screamed with laughter. Thank God, Benny thought: someone can scream.

As the bar grew noisier, Benny and Nan gazed at each other without tenderness, in the hard labor of separation. He felt the first wellsprings of hatred—liberating, a breeze from the soul's window. You have to hate them first if you're going to break up with them. Gathering himself, he nodded at her, stood up with what he hoped was quiet dignity, and left her with the bar bill. At the entryway, like Orpheus, he turned to see her one last time. Would she follow him or at least keep an eye on him as he walked away? Certainly not: she was gazing through the window glass toward the street, studiously ignoring his departure and, worse, wearing a grim smirk as she reached back down into her purse for her phone. She'd give this Thor the good news: free, now and forever. Free to be you and me! No more Benny! She didn't look up as she tapped the letters.

All night Benny fought the beast of jealous rage, and he drank. Four a.m. found him in a whiskey stupor, lying on the floor in his apartment, cursing Nan and contemplating creative bedlam.

By morning, he had acquired an atom-smashing headache. His brain was a particle accelerator, throwing off broken pieces of thought. He emptied the savings account meant to pay off his student loans, transporting the cash out of the bank in a brown grocery bag he'd brought with him. The oversaturated sunlight blazed down on his hair, and his car's interior smelled like a bakery oven. Back at home, cash in hand, he wrote a letter to the dean of admissions of the architecture school he had planned to attend in September, saying that he would *not* be arriving this fall, or ever. Then he called Dennis.

"Nan broke up with me," he announced.

"No kidding. How come?" his friend asked.

"This guy. She says she . . . I dunno. She fell in love with him or something. Law school guy. Love bloomed in the lecture hall. His name's Thor, if you can believe it."

"Too bad."

"Also he's a triathlete."

"A triple threat. How could you possibly compete with that?"

"Couldn't," Benny said. "I'm going to take all my money and gamble it away."

"That's a really good idea. An *excellent* idea. Where you going?"

"Phelps Lake. One of those Indian casinos. Hey, you want me to visit you first? This morning? How're you feeling?" Benny hadn't been over to the hospital for two days now.

"Naw. Go up to the casino and gamble all your money away and then call me or just come down here and give me the full rundown about how you're totally broke and ruined."

Benny's idea is that he's keeping his friend alive by sending out stories from the battlefield. Before he got sick, Dennis was a real player. In any particular room, if Dennis hadn't made a pass at an attractive woman, it was just an oversight. He had coached Benny in the complicated norms of seduction, separation, and betrayal.

Accordingly, Benny had loaded himself and his life savings into his rusting and dented Corolla and driven eighty-seven miles north on the interstate, past the antiabortion billboards and the federal prison in Sandstone, and now here he is, wearing a T-shirt, jeans, and sandals, a recent college grad playing blackjack at a casino staffed by Native Americans. He's bleary and hungover and soul-sick. The trouble is, he's on a lucky streak and has won three hundred dollars, and he just keeps winning. A curse is on him: he cannot lose. More people are gathering around to watch this desperate, bloodshot young man, and they're stupefied by his behavior. What they regard as a blessing, he believes is a catastrophe: look at the expression of dismay on his face as his winnings accumulate! Once in a while, the gates of the City of Ruination are closed to visitors. He knocks; he cannot get in.

Behind him, the casino zombies are living it up. Air thick with cigarette smoke and fetid hopelessness circulates dully around him, and the blinging electronic music from slot machines projects a kind of hypnotically induced amusement-park ruckus. Having won again on a double down, Benny backs up from the blackjack table and decides to survey the main floor. He will call Dennis later.

Ghouls smoking cigarettes drop tokens into the slots. The machines continue to sing their manic little robot ditties. Here and there, officials survey the operation, pretending that they are merely there to help. It's a low-rent casino, and the patrons are more humble than you might expect— shabbily dressed, glowering, half-mad with unrecoverable losses. An old couple, holding on to each other for stability, newly broke, shuffle past Benny and nod in a stubbornly friendly way to him, this being Minnesota. She's wearing a cap that says SAY HI TO GRANDMA! and his cap says GONE FISHIN'! A red-haired middle-aged woman at a slot machine to Benny's right labors away at losing money, and on her T-shirt are the words WHOA IS ME!

Behind him, a man speaks to a woman, probably his wife. They're both wearing wedding rings. "He looked like a faggot undertaker," the man says in a thick Minnesota accent, "and I know I'm half-right."

That does it. The spell breaks. The romance of self-destruction can only go on for so long, and it can't go on here among these politely unpleasant people. This isn't Las Vegas, a professionally designed entryway to Hell, where experienced Technicolor devils have been in comfortable residence for decades tossing Mom and Pop down into the pit. It's just lowly Phelps Lake, where small lives become slightly smaller. Time for Benny to go back to his life, to return to the cities, and drop in on Dennis.

He seems to have sobered up. His headache has gone away. He checks his watch.

Now he's standing near the entryway door, close to the last-chance slots, and is about to return to his car with his winnings when a man wearing a green tie over a white shirt approaches him with his hand out as if in greeting. The man's thinning hair is arranged in a halfhearted comb-over, and his eyeglasses sit on his nose at a tilt, the right lens lower than the left. He looks, it is fair to say, like a survivor of a plane crash dressed up to go on a talk show. On the approaching face is a Mr. Potato Head expression of rigid bonhomie.

"Hello, there. I saw you looking at me," the man says, shaking Benny's hand, "from across the crowded room, and you were wondering who I was. Who is that man, you were thinking."

"No," Benny says sourly. "I wasn't thinking that at all."

"It often happens," the man says, as his hand continues to shake Benny's. "People see me and it's like, 'I know that guy. Who *is* that guy? Is he famous?'"

"I didn't think that."

"Well, you will. I have one of those recognizable faces."

"I don't recognize it," Benny says. "Please stop shaking my hand."

"Will do," the man says cheerfully. "Do you recognize me now?"

"No."

"You could say I'm the greeter here." Finished with shaking, his hand returns to the man's side. "You could say that I'm the spirit of fun. Ha *ha*! I like for everybody to have the best possible time here at the Gray Wolf."

"I have to go," Benny tells him. "I have to get back."

"What's your hurry?" the man asks. "By the way, I'm Nathaniel Farber." Again the hand comes out, and, unthinkingly, Benny takes it. The shaking recommences. "I was in pictures." He waits. "The *movies*," he says, to clarify.

"Pleased to meet you." Benny pulls his hand away abruptly. "I have to go."

"Sometimes people say, 'Not *the* Nate Farber!' Usually they say that. Or they cry out with recognition."

"I must be the exception that proves the rule."

"They say, 'I saw you in *Moon over Havana*. And I saw you in *Too Many Cats!* You were so funny!'"

"Are those movies?"

"Major studio productions. One at Warner's, the other at Metro. Of course, that was some years ago." Fleetingly, the rictus dies on the face of the showbiz veteran. "What's your name, young fella?"

"Benny."

"And what brings you to our Gray Wolf Casino, Benny?"

"I was trying to lose my life savings. I was upset."

"And did you succeed, Benny?"

"I did not. I won a few hundred dollars."

"Goes to show, Benny, how unpredictable the future can be. The stars, dear Brutus, are not in ourselves. Would you like my autograph?"

"No, thank you." Nathaniel Farber's breath, floating like a soap bubble in Benny's direction, smells of mouthwash tainted with vodka.

"Are you leaving? Please stay. We here at the Gray Wolf feel that you haven't yet enjoyed yourself to the outer limit."

"Actually, I have an appointment, sort of, with someone in Minneapolis."

"A sort-of appointment? I never heard of such a thing."

"You have now."

"Who is she?"

"He. Not 'she.' He. His name's Dennis. He used to teach film at the university before he got sick. He'll know who you are. Excuse me, but I have to go."

"Why doesn't he teach film now?" Nathaniel Farber asks.

"He's dying," Benny tells him. "But I'll tell him all about you anyway."


On the way back, he runs into a rainstorm. The car shakes from side to side from the force of the crosswinds. Overhead, the clouds have a horror-movie look. On the freeway, cars coming in the opposite direction have their headlights on, and their windshield wipers are oscillating at high speed. Inside the cars, the drivers have the stricken I-was-there faces of trauma survivors. Soon enraged supercharged raindrops mixed with BB-size hail pelt the front windshield like liquid bullets, the impact sounding metallic as the projectiles hit the glass more forcibly with each mile, until the windows fog up, and Benny pulls over to a rest stop, where he waits out the storm.


"Guess who I saw at the Gray Wolf Casino?" Benny asks upon entering Dennis's hospital room. "Nathaniel Farber. The old actor. They hired him as an official greeter up there." He sits down next to the hospital bed, facing away from his friend, who does not like to be looked at in his present condition.

"No kidding. *Moon over Havana*. Billy Wilder used him once. He played a health inspector. Our grandparents' generation—he always reminded me of Gene Raymond. Just a minute, just a minute," Dennis says, staring at the TV set hanging from the ceiling. "*Storage Wars* is on. I gotta see what's in the locker." The gap in conversation allows Benny to examine his friend's face, which has grown gaunt. His eyes have that staring look. He wears a maroon-and-gold stocking cap.

"I won a few hundred dollars up there," Benny says. "I couldn't lose. By the way, where's your mom?"

"Downstairs in the cafeteria. She likes the hubbub. It's a contrast to here."

"How long will she be in Minneapolis?"

When Dennis doesn't reply, Benny turns to him and sees that his friend has fallen asleep, probably from the morphine. Or perhaps he's had a pain spasm. Benny reaches over and shuts off the TV set.

"Hold my hand," Dennis says, his eyes still closed. Benny takes Dennis's hand in his own, and they sit there for a moment in silence.

"Can you believe that she left me? For a law student?" Benny asks.

"Can you fucking believe *this*? I'm dying," Dennis says, with his eyes still closed. "I talked to my oncologist yesterday. He had just looked at the new X-rays. He said, and I quote, 'Dennis, if I told you your cancer hadn't spread, it'd be like saying that shit doesn't stink.'" He sighs. "He needs to practice his bedside manner. What happened to tact? Tell me again about what she said to you last night."

Benny tells him the story again: Nan's new guy, Thor, the runner, dedicated to practicing poverty law once he passes the Minnesota bar, has replaced Benny in her affections. Dennis's hand feels cold and dry in his own. Once again he seems to fall asleep. "I can't even think about architecture," Benny tells Dennis. "All I can think about is her. She's got me in her grip." Dennis nods. "Buddy, is there anything I can do for you?"

"Get the nurse," Dennis says. "I need more morphine. Like right now. Pronto."

Benny releases Dennis's hand and walks down to the nurses' station and tells the woman—Lucille, her name is—who's in charge of his friend that his friend is in pain again and needs more morphine immediately. Lucille says she'll be down in ten minutes, and Benny returns to room 530.

"You've been losing weight," Dennis says dreamily, before coughing uncontrollably. "So have I."

"I've been running. I gotta try to look good."

"You're going to end up like Nathaniel Farber, that line of thinking."

"Why?"

"Any man over the age of thirty-five who isn't overweight is a narcissist."

"That's kind of oversimplified."

"No, it isn't," Dennis says. "You met Nathaniel Farber, didn't you?"

"Don't leave me here," Benny tells Dennis, after a long silence. "Don't go away."

"Don't leave me here," Dennis repeats, holding his hand out for Benny to take. "Don't go away." After another long silence, during which they both hear a car horn honking out-side, Dennis asks, "What was her name again?"

"Nan."

"Oh, right. I introduced you to her."

"Yeah," Benny says. "I guess you did. At that party." If you invited Dennis to a party, he would always hold out on you, in case there might be a better party elsewhere.

"We had a thing," Dennis says. "Nan and me. For two weeks. I told you that. She was cute. Don't be offended, but I slept with her. I slept with all of them. Maybe that's why I got cancer. Or maybe it was the cocaine. There's a theory about cocaine and . . ." He winces. "It's all disinformation."

"But that was just lust, what you had," Benny says, want-ing to rouse Dennis to argumentation after another pause, with the hospital's ventilation system whirring in the back-ground. "What we had, Nan and I, well, that was *special.*"

That morning when Nan had made scrambled eggs in Benny's apartment kitchen, she had added salsa, and when she approached the kitchenette table where Benny was sit-ting, wearing only his boxer shorts underneath which his dick was again hardening to pay her tribute, she carried the serving plate toward him with a expression of the purest happiness and anticipation, and at that moment, though never afterward, she walked toward him looking like a gift, like all the colors of the rainbow. If that wasn't love, what else could it be?

"You're funny," Dennis says to Benny, as Lucille comes in, closing the curtain around Dennis momentarily. When she draws the curtain again, his face has relaxed somewhat.

"Well, there are other fish in the sea," Benny tells his friend. "That's the cliché with which I comfort myself. Other fish, other seas. I'll be feeling one hundred percent soon."

"You're funny."

"But I need coaching. From you."

"You're funny." Then he says, "You're going to be on your own in no time flat. Where's your hand?" Benny takes his friend's hand again.

"How come this?" Benny asks.

"I'm scared."

"Well, you have a right to be," Benny says, before he realizes how undiplomatic that is. "I only meant that . . ."

"I know what you meant."

"Sorry."

"Don't worry. Did I tell you . . . they found a hospice for me?"

"No. You didn't tell me."

"It's out in Hopkins. It's cheap. At last: a hospice I can afford. Where are the girls now?" Dennis asks. "Where have the girls all gone? I haven't had a lot of them visit me. Maybe they'll drop roses on my casket."

"They'll be here."

"Describe them. Do me a favor. Tell me a story. Let's fill the time."

"Well," Benny says. He tries to think of what would comfort his friend. A paradise, not of virgins but of experienced worldly women, funny, quick-witted, sharp-tongued women, moviegoers who know the difference between early and late Ozu, or Kurosawa, of the styles of screwball comedies, of Stanwyck saying, "I need him like the axe needs the turkey," but instead, sitting next to the bed and holding the hand of his friend, who seems now to be drifting into unconsciousness, he launches into a verbal dreamworld of tits and ass, blowjobs, ecstasy, a little touch of verbal porno here at the bedside, to keep his friend's spirits up, at least for a while.

# Sloth

For an hour the doctor could think of nothing worth doing and no reason to rise from his chair, so he sat in a corner of the coffee shop in downtown Minneapolis, four blocks away from the hospital, with the newspaper's sports section spread out in front of him, unread, the evening traffic outside going by with the characteristic hiss of tires on wet pavement, a sibilant personal sound like whispering. He gripped a double espresso but did not drink it. Wind gusts whipped the decorative downtown trees. That day on rounds he had checked in on one of his patients, a little girl whom he had diagnosed with Eisenmenger syndrome. She had developed endocarditis, an infection of the heart that had not been caught before some damage to the valves had occurred. This infection had been followed by a stroke. The family had gathered in the ICU's waiting area, and one aunt had said loudly to the assembled relatives that her niece, lying there, was *unrecognizable*, and the doctor could tell—from years of similar scenes—that she, the aunt, was eager to assign blame to someone, starting with the pediatrician (himself), and then advancing up the scale of responsibility, to the radiologist, the surgeon, and at last God. With each new step the accusations would grow more unanswerable. Nevertheless, the arias of blame would soon begin, and they would have their predictable and characteristic melodies of resentment, rage, and malpractice. They were unstoppable. The lawyers would accompany her and provide the harmonizing chorus. For now, thinking of his patient, Dr. Jones could not go home or move in any direction, and, once again, sitting with his back against the coffee shop's brick wall, the newspaper in front of him detailing the Twins' latest loss to the Royals, he considered pediatric medicine the very worst of all specialties, a curse upon every physician who had ever practiced it, a field that he should never have gone into and would like to quit for some other better job, like selling boats. People were unusually happy when buying boats. Boat salesmen were dispensers of cheer. By contrast, the observance of pediatric medicine put the insane cruelties of God fully on display. His teachers in medical school had warned him about these psychic difficulties, but they had not warned him sufficiently, and just today one of his colleagues asked him whether he had started "laying crepe" with the girl's relatives, doctor-talk referring to prepping family members for the patient's untimely demise.

He had been hoping that his friend Benny Takemitsu, the hack architect, might stop by the coffee shop on a break from his evening run, but there was no sign of him, so with great effort, Dr. Jones, who was a bit stout, at last found some resource of energy and rose from his chair and headed toward the Mississippi River, where lately he had been granted certain . . . visitations. The visitations were products of his exhaustion. He'd considered talking to his psychiatrist friend, Dr. Gloat—his actual name—about his hallucinatory visitors, but Gloat would probably prescribe an antipsychotic like clozapine or aripiprazole, part of that class of drugs that were chemically like a wrecker's ball set loose in the brain. Or he could call on another pal, a gerontologist, who might diagnose him with Lewy body dementia, an affliction that included voices and full-scale hallucinations of the sort that Dr. Jones had been experiencing. With a diagnosis like that, they'd put you in the bin. Despite his visitations, he recognized inwardly, as the spirals of intuition turned gently and logically, that he wasn't demented any more than he was psychotic. Nor was he delusional. He was just seeing things as the shamans once did, the holy men and women. He was becoming a holy man. Such a change was unprecedented in his professional experience. The prospect of going mad, or holy, did not seem to be that much of a catastrophe to him as long as he could keep calm while the specters appeared. Perhaps some bed rest would be indicated. The trouble with mad people was not the hallucinations or the garbled speech, but the panic they felt, which could be contagious and often created a vulgar effect among the villagers. Elijah Elliott Jones, M.D., considered himself a scientist. Scientists should remain calm, even if they become sanctified.

He ambled down Second Street past the Mill City Museum, facing Mill Ruins Park, where a grain mill had exploded a century ago and the rubble had been left more or less as it once was, for tourists to gawk at. The location was billed as the Cradle of Carbohydrates, and indeed the flour for American bread had been shipped out of here for decades: Gold Medal flour, Pillsbury's Best, all of them, although not anymore, manufacturing having gone global in search of cheap uninsured labor. The light had a peculiar shellacked quality this evening, with a surface glitter and sheen, as if designed for a movie. He made his way to the Stone Arch Bridge, built of limestone and granite in 1883 for use by the Great Northern railway. The Empire Builder himself, James J. Hill, had seen to its construction. Grain from the farms of the upper Midwest had arrived here on his railroad, had been stored in his silos along the river, and had been milled with the power of the Mississippi River at St. Anthony Falls. The riffraff railroad workers, their jobs finished, would drift toward the whorehouses and bars on Washington Avenue, but the riffraff had disappeared decades ago, along with their jobs, and Washington Avenue, following urban renewal, had gone upscale and pricey and was now full of spoiled and contemptible young professionals. Dr. Jones had almost seen the ghosts of the old workers, those tough sooty characters. He was very close to that realm. Tonight, before crossing the river, he took out his cell and called his wife, Susan, to say that he would be late in arriving home, but she had already gone to bed, and the doctor ended up speaking to their antique answering machine, the one with the microcassette. The doctor loved spunky defunct technologies. After having decided to stay on this side of the river, he chose a park bench in shadow some distance away from a sleeping bum stretched out on a bench next to the bum's cherished bag of discarded aluminum cans. The doctor sat and closed his eyes. He felt himself falling into the other world.


When he bothered to turn to his right, he noted that a silhouette had materialized next to him, the famous outline of the old filmmaker encased in layers of fat. The director's sadness and loneliness drifted up from his bulk like a corpulent mist in the still air. In his right hand he held a ghost cigar that produced ghost smoke. He wore a spotless dinner jacket, although he gave the impression of having been in the park for years, sitting there exposed to the elements. "I was wondering who it would be this time," Dr. Jones said. "But somehow I never expected to see you of all people here. Didn't they let you in? To heaven, or whatever they're calling it now . . . ?"

"Good evening," the director said, bending slightly toward Dr. Jones out of a habitually polite formality. His voice had the familiar sonorous rumble, mixed with audible memories of his Cockney upbringing. His face had an odd phosphorescence. "No, they didn't let me in. Not as yet. The rules are quite complex, you see. One must wait. There are pages of rules written with blood mixed in ink, thick volumes of these rules stretching from the floor to the ceiling, which is way up *there*, so high that no applicant has actually seen it. You can't imagine a room without a visible ceiling, and yet it must exist. Spiritual exercises are required, of a sort not dreamed of by the Jesuits of my youth. Those Jesuits would whip a boy's upraised hands, palms out, to intensify the pain. They enjoyed cruelty, some of those Jesuits," the old man said, with a trace of envy mixed with bitterness. "They were very clever in those days: they liked the boys to cower. They *quite* enjoyed it. It is a form of control, you understand, to cause someone to cower in fear. Fear supplied the voltage of their faith, and fear became their métier. So I was trained by masters. But as it turns out, one has to overcome . . .

certain tendencies. As at one time I was a director, now I am directed. Tell me, have you ever thought about suspense?"

"Your specialty," the doctor said.

"Yes, once." The director nodded sadly, out of a bottomless melancholy. "All that caring about what happens next." He waited. "Now nothing happens next." He took a puff from his cigar, and the exhaled smoke formed itself into the shape of a cat, which sauntered away in the night air.

"Why do they have you sitting out here, night after night? For months? Years?"

"Penitence," the director said. "I sit in the rain and snow observing the river. But that is not our subject. We were talking about suspense." The director looked over at Dr. Jones. "You could lose some weight," he said with a ghostly smile. "For the lifeboat movie I invented a nonexistent weight-reduction drug, Reduco, that you might want to try. But, yes, we were talking about suspense. For example, that homeless man over there—"

"Wait a minute," the doctor said. "How can I try Reduco if it doesn't exist?"

"The same way that you watch a movie about people who never walked the Earth. You swallow a pill containing dreams. Please don't interrupt. Anyway, that man who looks like a bum is actually in flight from people who are pursuing him for reasons that I shall disclose once I think of them. He is in disguise. He merely looks like a bum. Underneath the shabby clothes and three-day growth of beard is Cary Grant. Perhaps Cary Grant has possession of some secrets related to international negotiations, but I believe it is more likely—

yes, indeed I can now see it—that through a case of mistaken identity our friend here was targeted as a *terrorist* guilty of terrible, malicious sabotage that resulted in the darkening of an electrical grid covering much of the north-central United States. An accused saboteur, his face in all the newspapers. Did you know how easy it is to disable a nuclear reactor? No? A few broken valves, a bit of sand . . . And so here he is, our bum, hiding out, disguised, on the banks of the Mississippi River, accompanied by his grocery cart and bag of aluminum cans. But over there, just upstream, a mile away from where we sit, the true terrorist, whom we shall call the Arab, approaches, gripping his knife, intent on murder." The old man paused, savoring the doctor's interest. "The Arab approaches our scene with his knife blade out. The sharpened knife blade reflects the streetlight; it *shines*. And now misty rain begins to fall. The Arab has already killed others, in one instance just this morning at the Minneapolis Farmers Market in broad daylight, so that the victim's blood splashed all over the cauliflower and the yellow squash. Blood splattered everywhere on the produce, quite a mess to clean up. There will be a chase across the river, through the hydroelectric plant right down there, ending in the caves far underneath us, below, the caves of the Mississippi, the *endless* caves, where the Girl is tied up. I haven't mentioned the Girl, but she's down there now. Imagine her: a blond beauty knotted up with hemp. Imagine the rope *tight* around her wrists and her ankles. We already know about her, don't we? Beneath our feet resides an underground labyrinth, and there she is, our blonde. Her cries are piteous. We desire her, like oysters. An *endless* labyrinth. Cary Grant finds her, but the Arab approaches them both, with his knife. The movie will go on for days."

"That doesn't sound like you."

"Well, what *does* sound like me?"

The doctor thought for a moment. "'Mother...'" he recited. "'Mother... what is the phrase? ... Mother isn't quite herself today.'" The director nodded. After a moment, Dr. Jones thought of another line. "'And you know what else, Doctor? I don't think Mozart is going to help at all.'" This time the old man's face took on a downcast expression. The line seemed to cause him pain. "'That plane's dustin' crops where there ain't no crops,'" the doctor recited more happily, getting into the spirit of things.

"Stop," the old man commanded. "Cinema is not the writer's medium but the director's. All the same, none of those lines is my favorite." He sat waiting for the doctor to ask him the inevitable question, and when the doctor did so, the director answered, "'Do you know the world's a foul sty?'" After a pause, he said, "*That* was my favorite line. *I* wrote it. It's not Thornton Wilder's line; it's mine. Joe Cotten read it very well. Even the moronic masses got the point that time around."

"That's not a very nice line," the doctor said.

The old man shrugged in response. "Fuck nice. Do you know," he said, "that even now as we speak, your friend Benny Takemitsu is being mugged elsewhere, nearby, down by the Federal Reserve Building? The perpetrator of this crime is a young idealistic gay man who needs the money for painkilling drugs. He has assaulted this Takemitsu with a baseball bat. In the montage, the baseball bat hits the back of the knee, and we cut to Takemitsu's face, astonished with pain. Then in a medium shot, Takemitsu falls. Then we see in an insert the assailant's hand reaching for the victim's wallet. Your friend will be all right, however."

"How do you know?"

"The dead know everything," the director said. "But such knowledge does us no good: we cannot move from our fixed positions. Approaching death and then following it, the camera cannot move. The camera must . . . never move. For example, you were about to ask me if I would like to walk with you back to your car, for your trip homeward. I cannot. I must stay here on this bench of desolation until my penitence and contrition are complete. I must apologize to the Girl, the one at whom I threw all those birds. I made her a star. There are others to whom I must apologize once they reach this realm. According to the rules written in blood and ink, the rules that reach to the ceiling, I must feel the apologies inwardly. *That* is the hard part, the inward contrition. With respect to inward contrition, the Jesuits are no help."

"Why here? Why in Minneapolis?"

"The Girl was born here," the old man said, "and one's spirit always naturally returns to the place where one was born. For years I sat by the Thames in London. Now I'm here. I'm not always alone. Benny Herrmann sometimes comes down here to keep me company. We are reconciled, he and I. He wrote music for me. Did you know that he once lived in Minneapolis at the Nicollet Hotel, a few blocks away from here? He composed his opera, *Wuthering Heights,* a pastiche of Delius, in this city. I never liked it. Don't tell him.

However, most nights I have no company. So I make pictures in my head, as I used to do. And, now, you must leave me, Doctor. You cannot stay."

"Mr. Hitchcock," he asked, "will my patient die? The little one?"

"No, not this time," the director informed him. "There will be a miraculous recovery. In fact, it has already occurred. Her heart has somehow repaired itself, no one knows how, though perhaps your initial diagnosis of damage to the valves was mistaken. Why should anyone question such a recovery, such a miracle? No one ever does. They will not. Music up. We dissolve to happy, smiling faces. Joy abounds. The end, and the final credits," he said sourly. "Not like many of my pictures, but there you are. So for once, my dear doctor, you will have *a happy ending*. The scene in the hospital will be directed not by me but by Frank Capra. This case will bring you great renown. You will be cheered. A box-office smash hit, one might say if one were inclined to use such phrases. Henceforth you will be known as a healer with uncanny resources, like a shaman. Well, I must bid you a good night."

At that moment, the director himself dissolved, leaving behind the odor of cigar smoke and burnt coal. What was brimstone, actually? Just another name for sulfur, with a smell to wake you up, to make your eyes open in astonishment.

Dr. Jones rose from the bench and jammed his hat down on his head, lowering himself against the wind as he made his way to his car. Driving home, he saw the souls of the dead wandering about the city. They seemed not to see each other.

No one smiled. The dead seemed puzzled by their condition, distracted, preoccupied. They appeared to be dressed in nondescript clothes from Goodwill, although some were naked. Among them ran a few children. None of the women were pretty, or the men handsome. They were beyond all that. Some sat on park benches or stood in bus shelters next to actual living people. The dead were identifiable not because they were semitransparent but because they walked several inches above the ground, and they did not reflect light but radiated it, like fireflies.

If I am going mad, Dr. Jones thought, remembering Herzog, it's all right with me.

Once in the house, he touched the play button on the kitchen's message machine. A nurse from the hospital had called to say that Dr. Jones should phone the unit as soon as possible. Something strange and quite wonderful had happened. He trudged up the stairs feeling as if he had shed some weight.

On an impulse, instinctively negotiating his way through the nearly perfect dark, he knocked softly on his son's door before entering. Wearing his boxer shorts, Raphael lay sprawled not under the covers but on top of them, his seventeen-year-old body giving off a sweetly rank boy's smell, leathery and acidic like that of a horse's stable. The clock radio blinked on the bedside table, illuminating the poster over the bed of a superhero cheesecake girl who was apparently from another planet. She aimed a weapon-thing at the viewer. Her confrontational breasts pushed aggressively at her vinyl uniform. She had powerful thighs and the scowling face of an angel. Raphael's tae kwon do awards and cups gleamed and glowed from two shelves across from the window. Dr. Jones gazed at his boy for a minute in the near dark. He could not look at his son in daylight without Raphael saying, *"What?"* So he watched him now. Minutes passed.

After leaving his son's room, he knocked softly on his daughter's bedroom door before entering. Theresa had always been a light sleeper, and, when Dr. Jones entered her room, she awoke and blinked.

"Daddy," she yawned. She was still usually happy to see him, and she smiled absentmindedly now. "What are you doing in here?"

"Late night," he said. "I just got home."

"I was having a dream," she told him. "I was having it when you came in."

"A dream? About what?"

"It's private," she said. She was fourteen.

"Okay." He approached her, kissed her on her forehead, and turned around to leave. "Sleep well. Have more dreams, sweetie."

"Where have you been?" she asked. "There's that smell." She wrinkled her nose. She had a disobliging side. "You smell like . . ." But she appeared to have fallen asleep again before she finished the thought.

After leaving her room, Dr. Jones stood out on the second-floor landing waiting to go into his own bedroom, where he himself would soon be sleeping and where Susan was certainly sleeping now; he could hear her soft reassuring snores. His patient, the one who might actually be in recovery, having suffered a minor miracle, was named Da'neesha, and her mother had said that her daughter loved to dance and *wanted to grow up to help people.* He bowed his head. He tried to bless his family, his patients, all the afflicted everywhere in the world, but the blessing, being too large and weighing too much, and improbable besides, stayed with him and would not travel.

In the bedroom, he took off his clothes and got into bed next to his wife. Snuggling up behind her, he put his arm around her. When she made a noise, he whispered to her, "There's something I want you to do."

She made another noise.

"I want you to pray for me."

"Hmmm," she said.

"I don't understand anything," he whispered to her, "and I need to understand what's happening to me." The words would have sounded agitated if he had spoken them during the day, but it was nighttime, so what he said had no force, since the souls of the dead were still moving here and there outside his house on their endless pilgrimages, and they had made Dr. Jones sound nonsensical. Meanwhile, the doctor felt sleep overtaking himself so rapidly that he quickly forgot his request, and as he crossed the river and lost consciousness that night, he felt his own ghost arriving to embrace his body.

# Avarice

My former daughter-in-law is sitting in the next room eating cookies off a plate. Poor thing, she's a freeloader and can't manage her own life anywhere in the world. Therefore she's here. She's hiding out in this house, for now, believing that she's a victim. Her name's Corinne, and she could have been given any sort of name by her parents, but Corinne happens to be the name she got. It's from the Greek, *kore*. It means "maiden." When I was a girl, no one ever called me that— a maiden. The word is obsolete.

Everyone else under this roof—my son and his second wife (my *current* daughter-in-law, Astrid), and my two grandchildren—probably wonders what Corinne is doing here. I suppose they'd like her to evaporate into what people call "thin" air. Corinne's bipolar and a middle-aged ruin: when she looks at you, her vision goes right through your skin and internal organs and comes out on the other side. She mutters to herself, and she gives off a smell of rancid cooking oil. She's unpresentable. If she tried to go shopping alone at the supermarket, the security people would escort her right back out, that's how alarming she is.

The simple explanation for her having taken up residence here is that she appeared at the downtown Minneapolis bus depot last week, having come from Tulsa, where she lived in destitution. She barely had money for bus fare. My son, Wesley, her ex-husband, had to take her in. We all did. However, the more honest explanation for her arrival is that Jesus sent her to me.

Two weeks ago I was in the shower and felt a lump in my breast. I actually cried out in a moment of fear and panic. Then my Christian faith returned to me, and I understood that I would be all right even though I would die. Jesus would send someone to help me get across into the next world. The person He sent to me was Corinne. I know that this is an unpopular view among young people, but there is a divinity that shapes our ends, and at the root of every explanation is God, and at the root of God is love.

I go into the room where Corinne resides, knitting a baby thing. I pick up the cookie plate. "Thank you, Dolores," she says. She gazes at me with her mad-face expression. "Those were delicious. I've always loved ginger cookies. Is there anything I can do for you?" she asks. She's merely being polite.

"Soon," I tell her. "Soon there will be."


You get old, you think about the past, both the bad and the good. You have time to consider it all. You try to turn even the worst that has happened into a gift.

For example, my late husband, Mike, Wesley's father, was killed by the side of the road as he was changing a tire. This was decades ago. He was the only man I ever married. I never had another one, before or after. A rich drunk socialite, a former beauty queen fresh from a night of multiple martinis with her girlfriends, her former sorority sisters, plowed right into him. Then she went on her merry way. Well, no, that's not quite right. After she hit Mike, my husband's body was thrown forward into the air, and then she ran over him, both the car's front and rear tires. Somehow she made her way home with her dented and blood-spattered car, which she parked in the three-car garage before she tiptoed upstairs and undressed and got into bed next to her businessman husband. She clothed herself in her nightgown. She curled up next to him like a good pretty wife. The sleepy husband asked her—this is in the transcripts—how the evening had gone with her girlfriends, if they had had a good time. Why was she shivering? She said the girls had been just fine but she was cold now. She didn't know that someone had gotten her license plate number, but somebody had, as her dark blue Mercedes-Benz sped away. A man out walking his dog on a nearby sidewalk wrote it down. God put him there—the dog, too.

Meanwhile, right after that, the police arrived at our house. I remember first the phone call and then the doorbell that woke my son, Wesley, in the crib that he was beginning to outgrow. He could climb right out of it but rarely did. Wesley began crying upstairs, while in the living room the police, who would not sit down on the sofa, gave me the bad news. My husband, Mike, they told me, was laid out in the morgue, alone, and I would have to identify him the next day. They were quite courteous, those two men, bearing their news. They spoke in low tones, hushed, which is hard for men. One of them wore old-fashioned tortoiseshell glasses. They warned me that I might not recognize my husband right away. But the next morning I did recognize him because of what he was wearing, a blue patterned sport shirt I had bought at Dayton's on sale and had wrapped up for him at Christmas. He had thanked me with a kiss on the lips Christmas morning after he opened it. "God Rest You Merry, Gentlemen" was playing on the radio when he did that. So of course I remembered the shirt.

The socialite testified that she didn't know she had hit anything or anybody. Or that she didn't *remember* hitting anything or anybody. There was some question—I heard about this—whether she had asked her stepson to take the rap for her. She wanted him to go straight to police headquarters and to say *he* had been driving his stepmother's car, drunk, at the age of seventeen, and therefore he would be tried as a minor and let off scot-free. He wouldn't do it. He wouldn't lie. The socialite's out of prison now, but my husband is still under the ground in Lakewood Cemetery.

I await the resurrection of the dead the way other people await weekend football. I'm old now, and the glory will all be revealed to me soon enough. I can feel it coming. Glory will rain down, soaking me to the skin.

If the socialite hadn't gone to prison, I imagined buying a handgun and going over there to her mansion and shooting her in cold blood if she answered the door. But, no, that's wrong: I had Wesley to raise, so I don't suppose I would have actually committed murder, though to kill her was extremely tempting, and the temptation did not come from Satan but from somewhere else inside me. It was mine. I dreamed of murder like a teenager dreaming of love. Peaceful and calm though I usually am, my husband's death and my wish for revenge changed me. Murder dwelt in my heart. Imagine that! It came as a surprise to me as I did the laundry or cooked dinner or washed dishes. Sometimes I wish I were more Christian: even now, at my age, with knees that hurt from arthritis and a memory that sometimes fails me, I still think certain people should be wiped off the face of the Earth, which is counter to the teachings of Jesus.

But what I'm saying is that Jesus intervened with me. He came to me one night and said, in that loving way He has, "Dolores, what good would it do if you murdered that foolish woman? It would do you and the world no good at all. It wouldn't bring Mike back. Turn that cheek," He said to me as I was praying, and of course I could see He was right. So I forgave that woman, or tried to. On my knees, I turned the other cheek as I wept. I turned it back and forth.

I believe that humanity is divided into two camps: those who have killed others, or can imagine themselves doing so; and those for whom the act and the thought are inconceivable. Looking at me, you would probably not think me capable of murder, but I found that black coal in my soul, and it burned fiercely. I loved having it there.

All my life, I worked as a librarian in the uptown branch. A librarian with the heart of a murderer! No one guessed.

Months after Mike's death, I'd go into Wesley's room to tuck him in at night. By then he was talking. "Where's Daddy?" he would ask me. Gone to heaven, I'd tell him, and he'd ask, "Where's that?" and I wanted to say, "Right here," but such an answer would be confusing to a child, so I just hummed a little tune, a lullaby to calm him. But my son knew there was something wrong with my face in those days, because of the hard labor of my grief. I didn't smile when I put my son to bed, and probably I didn't smile in the morning, either. I couldn't smile on my own. So there, at night, in his bed, he would get out from under the sheet, stand up in his rocket-ship-pattern pajamas, and he would raise his hand with his two fingers, the index finger and the middle finger outstretched in a V-for-victory sign. He would raise those fingers to the sides of my mouth, lifting them up, trying to get me to smile. He held his fingers there until I agreed to look cheerful for his sake. He was only a little boy, after all.

Time passes. The socialite, as I said, is out of jail, and Wesley has grown up and has two children of his own, my dear grandchildren, Jeremy and Lucy. Corinne gave birth to Jeremy before she fled the marriage, and Astrid, Wesley's second wife, gave birth to Lucy. But I still think of that woman, that socialite, driving away from my dying husband, and of what was going through her head, and what I've decided is that (1) she couldn't take responsibility for her actions, and (2) if she did, she would lose the blue Mercedes, and the big house in the suburbs, and the Royal Copenhagen china, and the Waterford crystal, and the swimming pool in back, and the health club membership, and the closet full of Manolo Blahnik shoes. All the money in the bank, boiling with possibility, she'd lose all that, and the equities upping and downing on the stock exchange. How she was invested! How she must have loved her *things*, as we all do. God has a name for this love: *avarice*. We Americans are running a laboratory for it, and we are the mice and rats, being tested, to see how much of it we can stand.

God's son despised riches. His contempt for riches sprouts everywhere in the Gospels. He believed that riches were distractions. Listen to Jesus: "You shall love your neighbor as yourself." If that isn't wisdom, I don't know what is. And remember this, about those who are cursed? "For I was hungry, and you gave me no food, I was thirsty and you gave me no drink, I was a stranger and you did not welcome me, naked and you did not clothe me."

Anyway, that's why Corinne is here. We have to feed and clothe her. Jesus doesn't believe in those glittering objects that hypnotize you. Hypnotized, you drive away from a dying man stretched out bleeding on the pavement.

I go into Corinne's room. She sits near the window with sunlight streaming in on her hair, which looks greasy, and she's talking before she even sees me. Apparently she's psychic and knows I'm coming. Since I'm not about to waste a beautiful morning like this one by brooding about breast cancer, I ask her, "Do you want to take a walk?" The question interrupts her monologue. "I've got to exercise these old bones," I tell her. Actually, I'm not *that* old. I'm in my seventies. It's just an expression.

She's gesticulating and carrying on a private conversation and seems to be very busy. Finally she says, "No, I don't think so."

"My joints hurt," I tell her. "I need some fresh air. And I need company." Craftily, I say to her, "Without a companion, I might fall down. I might not get back up. You never know."

"Oh, all right," she says, her nursing instinct rising to

one of her many surfaces. Even crazy people want to help out. "Oh all right all right all right." She puts on a pair of tennis shoes that Wesley bought for her yesterday, and we set out into the residential Minneapolis autumn, with me slightly ahead of her so that I don't have to smell her. Has she forgotten how to bathe? She's had opportunities here, bathtubs, showers, and soap—running water, both hot and cold. We amble down toward Lake Calhoun. Out on the blue waters of the lake, some brave fellow has one of those sailboard things and is streaking across the surface like a human water bug. Here onshore, the wind agitates the fallen leaves, whipping them around. It's October. My hips are giving me trouble today, and of course the lump in my right breast still remains there, patiently hatching.

"Do you think of the past?" she asks me. "I do. I wanted to call you on the telephone, you know," Corinne tells me, suddenly lucid, "once I moved away, after Jeremy was born. All those years ago. But I couldn't. I was a mess. I was ashamed of myself. I'm a heap of sorry."

"Oh, I didn't mind," I say, before I realize that she might misunderstand me. "We thought you were in a state." Then she tells me that she suffered panic attacks as a young mom—did I remember this? Of course I did—and that all she could do was escape from here, from the marriage and the child and the house. It's her old story. She repeats it all the time. Contrition is a habit with her now.

"Nature tricked me," she says. "I gave birth to a baby boy, and I didn't love him, and I was so ashamed of myself that I left town. I went to work in Tulsa in an emergency room," she says, knowing I know all this, "and I worked there for years, and the people came in night after night, and, Dolores, you can't imagine these poor people, knifed and shot and slashed and choked. Their hands were broken and their mouths were bloody and bullet holes pierced them, and some of them had been poisoned, and the rest of them were bent over and groaning, and you know what happened then?"

"You forgave yourself?" I ask. I wish she would change the topic. I wish she wouldn't dwell on any of this. She doesn't know I'm capable of murder.

"No. I lived with it. I saw things. I heard things. I got bloodied with the blood of strangers all over me. People screamed right into my face from pain and confusion. I saw a woman whose boyfriend had forced her mouth open and made her swallow poison. A person shouldn't see such terribleness. Her stomach had started to burn away before we got to her. When the police questioned the boyfriend, he said that she had told him to go fuck himself and that no woman was going to speak to him that way without consequences. So he did what he did. A manly thing to do. He had her name tattooed on his arm. With a heart! She survived that time, somehow. Two months later he killed her with a knife while she was sleeping. At least he was done away with in prison, later on, stabbed in turn. I think they call that karma. Thank goodness!"

By now we have made our way to Thirty-Sixth and to the fence surrounding the cemetery, whereupon Corinne loses her train of thought, as she does in all the subsequent walks we take together. When she collects her thoughts, she says, out of nowhere, "I hate them."

"Who?" I ask.

"Capitalists," she says, and suddenly I'm not following her. "They've made my life miserable. They've made me a crazy person. You can talk about the victims of Communism all you want, but as a woman I'm a victim of Capitalism, because did I tell you how they took away my pension? I had a pension, and they gave it to investors and the investors invested the money in bogus real estate and bundled something-or-others, and so I ended up with nothing, bereft, broke, a ruined person, no pension, plus I was crazy and alone, and meanwhile the capitalists were accumulating everything and coming after me in their suits. Have you ever seen how they live? It's comical."

"I agree with you, Corinne," I tell her, because I do. By now we are inside the cemetery, and we stop, because overhead in the sunlight a bird is singing, a song sparrow. We walk on quietly until we come to my husband, Mike's resting place.

Michael Erickson
1937–1967

Next to him is the space in the sacred ground where I'll be casketed in a couple of years. I love this cemetery. I do. I come here often. It's so quiet here under the balding blue sky with its wisps of white hair, and as we're looking down at the grass and the leaves, serenaded by the song sparrows, Corinne falls to her knees, smelly as she still is, a human wreck. She mumbles a prayer. "Wesley's daddy," my former daughter-in-law cries out, "God bless him, rest in peace, forever and ever and ever." She's so vehement, she sounds Irish.

This is how I know she'll take care of me once I'm inca-pacitated. Slowly, on my bad knees, I get down too. How lovely is her madness to me now.

We get back to the house, and that night the capitalism theme starts up again at the dinner table. We seem to be a house-hold of revolutionaries. This time it comes from Jeremy, who before dinner walks into the kitchen barefoot, holding his iPhone. I am sitting, drinking tea. He's sixteen or seventeen, I can't remember which. Usually he and I talk about space aliens, and I pretend they exist to humor him and bring him around eventually to Jesus, but tonight he's looking at something else. He's wearing his Rage Against the Machine T-shirt, and I notice that he's growing a mustache and suc-ceeding with it this time.

"I can't fucking believe it," he says to me. I don't mind his use of obscenity. Really, I don't. It tickles me, I can't say why. "Grandma Dee, do you like elephants?"

"I like them very much," I say. "Though I've never known any one of them personally." We're seated at the kitchen table. Astrid is making dinner, Wesley is in the garage doing something-or-other, and Corinne is upstairs cooing in front of the TV set. I don't know where Lucy is—reading some-where in the house, I expect. "They are among the greatest of God's creatures," I say. "I understand that they mourn their dead."

"So look at this fucking thing," he says, pointing at the little phone screen.

"It's too small. I can't see it."

"Want me to read it?" he asks. What a handsome young man he is. I enjoy his company. It's so easy to love a grandchild, there's no effort to it at all. Besides, his face reminds me of my late husband's face just a little.

"Sure," I say.

"Well, see the thing is, it's about elephants being killed and like that."

"What about them?" Astrid asks, from over by the stove. "Killed how?"

"Okay, so in Zimbabwe, which I know where it is because we've studied it in geography, anyway what this says, this article, is, they've been, these people, these Zimbabweans, putting cyanide into the water holes in this, like, huge park, to kill the elephants. And these fuckers have access, I guess, to industrial cyanide that they use in gold mining—"

"Jeremy, please watch your language," Astrid says demurely. She's dicing tomatoes now.

"And they've been, I mean the poisoned water hole has been, like, killing the little animals, the cheetahs, and then the vultures, that *eat* the cheetahs once they're dead, so it's, like, this total outdoor death palace eatery, but mostly the cyanide in the water holes has been killing the *elephants*." He gazes at me as if I'm to blame. I'm old. I understand: old people are responsible for everything. "Which are harmless?"

"Why've they been doing that?" I ask.

"Killing elephants? For the ivory. They have, like, tusks."

"How many elephants," I ask, "did they do this to?"

"It says here eighty," Jeremy tells me. "Eighty dead elephants poisoned by cyanide lying in dead elephant–piles. Jesus, I hate people sometimes."

"Yes," I say. "That's fair."

"What do you suppose they do with all that ivory?" Astrid asks, stirring a sauce.

"For carvings," I say. "They carve little Buddhas. They kill the elephants and carve the happy Buddha. Then they sell the happy Buddha to Americans. The little ivory Buddha goes in the lighted display case."

"That is so wrong," Jeremy says. "People are fucking sick. These elephants are more human, for fuck's sake, than the humans."

"It's the avarice," I say.

"It's the what?" he asks.

"Another word for greed. Go ask Corinne," I tell him. "She's upstairs, watching TV. She doesn't like it, either. She sounds like you."

"I still hate her," he says. "I can't talk to her yet. It's my *policy*. She just wasn't—"

"I know, I know," I say. "The policy is understandable. You'll just have to give it up eventually, sweetie."

"You can't tell me that it's no biggie because it was a biggie. If that wasn't a biggie, leaving my dad and you to take care of me, then nothing is big, you know?"

"Yes," I say. "I understand. For now."

"Jeremy," Astrid pipes up from the stove, "where's your father?"

"Him? He's out in the garage. He's working on the truck or something. I heard him drop his wrench and swear a minute ago. *There are too many of them in the house.* That's what he said before he went out there. He's *been* saying it."

"Too many what?" Astrid asks.

"Women," I say, because I know Wesley and how he thinks. "We confuse him."

I can see it all, and I know exactly what will happen. I have second-sight, which I got from my own father, who foresaw his death. He saw an albino deer cross the road in front of his car while he was on vacation, and he turned to my mother and said, "Something will happen to me," and something did. A stroke took him a week later, and no one was surprised.

They'll do surgery on me and give me the usual chemo and radiation. I'll be okay for a while, but then it will come back in other locations in my body. I won't have too much time then. The point is not to be morbid but to meet the end of life with celebration. This is what I want to say: the thought of dying is a liberation for me. It frees us from the accumulations.

This is where Corinne comes in. I have it all planned out. I will say to her, "There's something I want you to do. I want you to accompany me on this journey as far as you can. You can't go all the way, but you can keep me company part of the way." She'll agree to this. As long as I can walk, Corinne will take me around to the parks and the lakes. We'll go to the Lake Harriet rose garden, and together we'll identify those roses—floribunda! hybrid tea!—and then we'll stroll into the Roberts Bird Sanctuary nearby. I know most of the birds over there: there's a nest of great horned owls, with a couple of owlets growing up and eating whatever the mama owl brings to them, including, I once saw, a crow. I've seen warblers and egrets and herons, very dignified creatures, though comical. We'll see the standard-issue birds, the robins, chickadees, blue jays, and cardinals, birds of that ilk.

She'll take me over to the Lake Harriet Band Shell, where on warm summer nights the Lake Harriet Orchestra (there is one) will play show tunes, and I'll sit there in my wheelchair tapping along with "On the Street Where You Live."

We'll go down to the Mississippi, and we'll walk, or I'll be wheeled, along the pathways near the falls where the mills once were. I'll hear the guides saying that Minneapolis has a thriving industry in prosthetic medicine because so many industrial accidents occurred here years ago thanks to the machinery built for grinding, lost arms and so on, chewed up in the manufacturing process.

We'll be out on the Stone Arch Bridge, and Corinne will be absented in her usual way, ideas batting around her head, all the bowling pins up there scattered and in a mess. "I just don't have any filters," she'll say. "Any thought seems to be welcome in my brain at any time, day or night."

"Yes," I'll agree. I'll see the Pillsbury A Mill from here. What a comfort these old structures will be to us, still standing, their bright gray brick almost indestructible. Spray from the Falls of St. Anthony, named by Father Hennepin himself, will lightly touch my face, and I'll feel a sudden stab of pain in my body, but it won't matter anymore. Pain is the price of admission to the next world. Here will come a boy on a skateboard talking on his cell phone, and behind him, his girlfriend, also on a skateboard (pink, this time), texting as she goes. They'll look just born, those two, out of the egg-shell yesterday.

"Jeremy has one of those," Corinne will say, meaning the skateboard.

"He's quite the expert."

A fat man in flip-flops will pass by us. He'll be carrying several helium balloons, though I don't think they'll be for sale. On the other side of the bridge in Father Hennepin park, we'll rest under a maple tree. A single leaf will fall into my lap.

Here. I place it before you.

Glory, gloriousness. During my life, I never had the time to look closely at anything except Wes, when he was a baby, and my husband's headstone after he was gone. Now I'll have all the time in the world. Nothing will bore me now. My obliviousness will sink into my past history. Henceforth my patience will be endless, thanks to the brevity of time. Still-ness will steal over me as I study the world within. When I look down into my lap, I'll see in this delicate object the three major parts, with their branching veins, and the ten points of the leaf, and the particular bright red-rust-gold color, but it's the veins I'll return to, so like our own, our capillaries.

I'll finger the maple leaf tenderly and wonder why we find it beautiful and will answer the question by saying that it's God-given.

"There's that nice Dr. Jones, way over there," Corinne will say. "Lucy's doctor, out on a stroll." She'll pause, then say, "He could lose some weight."

"They're doing a Katharine Hepburn revival at the St. Anthony Main movie theater," I'll say, gazing at the marquee listing *Bringing Up Baby*.

"I always found her rather virile," Corinne will reply.

Thus will our days pass. You need a companion for what I'm about to do, and she'll be mine. Once I'm in bed, and then in the hospice, she'll read to me: *Pride and Prejudice*, my favorite book after the Bible, and she'll read from the Bible too, in her haphazard way, wandering from verse to verse. I wonder if she'll read from the Book of Esther, which never mentions God. Slowly I'll depart from this Earth, medicated on morphine as I will be, mulling and stirring the fog descending over me, over Elizabeth Bennet and Mr. Darcy, over daytime and its dark twin, night, while in the background someone will be playing Mozart on a radio. What is that piece? I think I'll know it. *Eine kleine Nachtmusik*, is it . . . ? Then I'll know more pain, and darkness. And then the light won't go on ever again, here.

On the other side I'll float for a while, between worlds. The pain will be gone, the pleasure, too, those categories neutralized. On all sides the boundary markers will have softened. Instead of coming from a single source, sound—music—will come from everywhere, and I'll hear it with more than my ears. I'll see with more than my eyes. Faces, I think, will pass me in corridors that are not corridors. The old vocabularies will be useless. They will name nothing anymore. This is the afterlife: we will be headed everywhere and nowhere, and we will drink in light, swallow it, swim in it. We'll hear laughter. And then—but "then" has no meaning—my dear Michael will find me, without his former shape but still recognizable, and he'll take my hand and lead me toward two rooms, and he'll say to me, "Oh, my dearest, my life, there is only one question, but you must answer it." And I'll ask him, "What is that question? Tell me. Because I love you . . ." I'll want to answer it correctly. What has this to do with the two rooms? But for that moment, after he puts his finger to his lips, he dissolves into air, he becomes pollen, and is scattered.

Somehow I am led into the first room. I'll be in a chamber of perpetual twilight. No one predicted this twilight, or the shabbiness, the feeling of a beggar. How richly plain this all is! Something wants something from me here. My attention. My love.

Now I'll enter the second room. And all at once I'll be dazzled: because here on the richest of thrones, gold beyond gold, sits this beautiful man, the most beautiful man I have ever seen, smiling at me with an expression of infinite compassion. His hair will be curling into tendrils of vibrating color. He will be holding up his palm, facing toward me, and in that hand I will see the world, the solar system, and the universe, rotating slowly. Behind him somehow are the animals, the great trees, everything.

It will be a test, the last one I will ever have. Which room do I choose?

The beautiful man clothed in light will ask me, "Do you admire me? Care for me?"

And I will say, "No, because you are Lucifer." And I will return to the room where it is always twilight, where all that is asked of me is love.

# Gluttony

Immediately after the accident, the doctor thought: *Stupid pain. Stupidity itself.* Below the knee, thanks to a fractured tibia, pain sent its dull, insistent neurological message upstairs. Pleasure never works that way. Pleasure's vague fog spreads underneath the skin in a warm narcotic glow—a fog that lights up the soul. Then it fades. You try to locate its source, and when you do, you crave more of it. The bottle. The drug. The woman. The meal. *Especially* the meal.

He found himself in the car eating beef jerky and the contents of a jumbo bag of potato chips. He didn't remember buying either one, but he must have purchased them when he stopped at the gas station. There, under the buzzing fluorescent lights, everyone had the doughy complexion of figures in a Hopper painting. Now, lying voluptuously on the front seat next to him, the bag of potato chips had been slit open in a kind of physical invitation into which he inserted his hand and withdrew food. Who had opened these packages? Someone had. *He* had, the doctor, Elijah. Who else? He didn't *remember* opening them; they had commanded him to make the first move, like the cake in *Alice in Wonderland* with the note attached: "Eat me." The food carried some responsibility for his excesses. It had desires, especially the desire to be consumed.

As he chewed and swallowed, he piloted the little car homeward through the dark. The steering wheel, however, was greasy with salt and cooking oils and saturated fats transferred from his palm, and although he wiped his fingers on his trouser leg, he couldn't get the grease off his skin. He felt drowsy. A literate man who entertained himself by reading Shakespeare, the doctor thought of Lady Macbeth: "What, will these hands ne'er be clean?" No, not these hands.

Against his own obesity, he had concocted his own diet plan, the Jones Plan. It was simplicity itself: every time you go into a restaurant, you order an entrée you do not want to eat. You don't like the taste of pork? You order pork. If the very sight of lobster disgusts you, you order lobster. You search the menu for an unpalatable culinary miscalculation, and then you request it. You ask your wife to prepare distasteful meals. The whole point is to be presented, day after day, with the unwanted. Naturally your wife is horrified and insulted by these ideas, when she does not regard them as comical. So far, however, no weight has been lost by anyone, thanks to the plan.

He pulled up into the driveway and wiped his hands again but this time on the car's dashboard. The lights were blazing inside the house, so Susan would still be up, vigilant about his arrival. When he stepped out of the car, he stood for a moment underneath the linden in the front yard and thoughtfully noted its seeds scattered on the lawn, pale green against the darker green of the grass illuminated by the streetlight. He felt a pain in his chest, and its attendant breathlessness. *Ah,* he thought, *it's that again.*

Inside the house, dressed in her blue bathrobe, Susan put

down her book, a history of the Armory Show, and rose to greet him. Her perfume preceded her. She kissed him, her eyes still on the door through which he had entered, a kiss both perfunctory and ironic, gestural in its well-meaning sweetness. "Your lips taste of salt," she said.

"Snack food," the doctor said. "I didn't really have dinner."

"Well, I could always heat up something for you. Are you still hungry? There's some leftover roast in the icebox." She enjoyed using antiquated words. "Or I could throw together a salad for you." She refused to follow the Jones Diet Plan and had said so. He shook his head. "Hey, guess what's going on here?" She gave him a brief and almost unreadable smile.

"I have no idea."

"We need to go to the basement." She waited. "We have to go down *there* if I'm going to tell you what's going on *here*." She cocked her head at the ceiling. "He might be listening."

"Rafe?"

"Who else?"

The doctor smelled a trace of gin on his wife's breath. She gave off an air of late-night melancholy elegance, an effect always intensified by alcohol, both the melancholy and the elegance. As she made her way toward the basement door entrance, her slippers shuffled on the linoleum, and her hips under the bathrobe swayed a little, a touch of womanly swagger intensified by the gin. Her expensively cut hair was streaked with gray, and her hair swayed with the same rhythm as her hips. He didn't want the younger version of Susan back—he did not desire younger women and despised men of his age who did—because a younger woman would leave him alone and untended in middle age, and he wanted to share the process of aging with someone, and not just any-body, but with her.

He felt his love flaring up for her: he remembered exactly how beautiful she looked when they first met years ago in San Francisco and saw how she appeared to the world now, the result of what their lives together had done to her, and the two versions of her, the young and the . . . well, she wasn't *old*, exactly, *weathered* was maybe a better word, touched him with an electric intensity that made it hard for him to breathe. How he loved her! He even loved her sadness. But loving your wife's sadness was a soul-error. Everyone said so.

She flipped on the light for the basement stairs and descended slowly, turning her feet at an angle so that she wouldn't slip on the narrow steps. At the bottom she flicked on another light. He followed her, trying to see the stairs over the mound of his belly. Her canned preserves lined the shelves behind her, fresh this past summer from the cauldron of the pressure cooker, including the stewed tomatoes in mason jars that sometimes started to ferment and caused the jars to explode. He remembered reading the paper one eve-ning and hearing a canned-tomato bomb go off underneath him. When he had gone downstairs to inspect the damage, shards of glass and stewed tomatoes were strewn all over the basement floor. It looked like a crime scene.

"How was your day?" she asked without interest. "Any hallucinations?"

"No. Just the usual can of worms." He was puffing from the exertion. At last he shrugged. "No. A little *better* than the usual worms."

"Remind me," she said, "to have someone come down here and inspect this place for mold. I smell mold."

"Okay." He noticed that she faced slightly away from him, though her right hand played with the fingers of his left hand, an old habit. She toyed with his wedding ring. He often felt that she was inspecting him.

"What's this about?" he asked, as the furnace rumbled to life. "How come we're down here?"

"What's *what* about?"

"Why we're down here."

"Oh. Down here?" She had grown terribly absentminded. Maybe it was the gin. "Oh, yes, of course." She nodded, a bit too forcefully, though she was still facing away from him. "Okay, so brace yourself. It seems that we were grandparents for, I don't know, about four weeks. Well, I mean, virtual grandparents, because, well, you get the picture."

"I do? No, I think I don't get the picture. What picture is this? Does this have to do with Jupie?"

"Bingo." She nodded and then wiped her eyes on her bathrobe sleeve. Jupie was their son's girlfriend—though "Jupie" was Eli and Susan's private name for this girlfriend whose actual name was Donna. A serious martial artist in tae kwon do, Rafe also considered himself a Marxist and had met this girl at a downtown political rally for voting rights or whatever. She was a freshman at Macalester, and although she was a year older than he was, her political activism matched his. They had hooked up soon after they met, and she had attended his matches and cheered him on. An attractive young woman with long brown hair, big brown eyeglasses to match, and a habit of chewing on her lip after she said anything, she nevertheless had an essential blurriness to her, which had provoked the doctor, after one of her visits to the house when she and their son had engaged him in conversation about gender identity, to call her Jupiter, not because she was godlike but because she resembled a gas planet. You'd go down through the layers of gas with her, and you never got to anything solid.

Her well-meaning earnestness had a certain charm. All it lacked was specific content.

By contrast, Rafe was all specific content. His body had a wiry density: when he moved, he seemed not to walk but to float, his movements all perfectly coordinated. When sparring, he showed absolutely no mercy, and his face showed an utter lack of expression. Watching him, his father felt pride and wonder. Well, he himself had been a fighter once.

Of course teens were hazy because life was still hazy to them, but this Donna, this Jupiter, was a mistress of the unspecific. Political platitudes and unsubstantiated generalizations just came leaking out of her. Besides, their son was still in high school, a senior. Big political rhetoric turned him on.

"Actually," Susan said, "we've got to stop calling her that. Her name's Donna. If Rafe ever catches us calling her Jupie again, he'll pitch a fit."

"So . . ."

"So I guess he forgot about condoms one time, or they got careless, but anyway he got her knocked up, unbeknownst to us, and also, equally unbeknownst to us, they went off to Planned Parenthood last week." This sentence came out of

Susan in pieces, severed into parts. Elijah took his wife into his arms and felt his old damaged heart breaking again, momentarily. "After all," his wife said into his shirt, "she's eighteen. Or nineteen. Old enough anyway to get an abortion."

"When did he tell you?"

"This evening. And here's the thing. He's been crying all afternoon. The poor kid. His crying is contagious. And . . . I don't know. You don't expect a tough young man to be torn up about it. You don't expect the fathers to cry."

"You don't?" He waited. "*I* do."

She just looked at him, through the tears.

"But anyway Rafe's not generic," he said. "He's not one of 'the men.' He's not one of 'the fathers.' Rafe is himself. Of course he'd cry. Jesus, the poor kid."

"I'd rather," she said, stiffening, "I'd rather you didn't lecture me about him. I believe that I know him as well as you do." She paused for effect. "If not better."

The doctor still held on to her. "Let's not fight," he said. "What should I do? Should I go talk to him?"

"Yes, but don't lecture him, okay?"

"I *don't* lecture."

"Of course you do. You hold forth. You get started, and once you get going, you're like an oscillating fan. Wisdom spews out of you in all directions."

Sorrow had made her cruel this evening. The doctor felt hungry again, terribly hungry, mealless, and he removed his bulky arms from where they had been encircling his wife and dropped them to his sides.

He trudged upstairs to sit with his son. At the top, he stopped for breath. He would sit down on Rafe's unmade bed, where conception had recently taken place. On the walls and shelves above them, the trophies and medals for his tae kwon do competitions would be on display. The smell of teenage boy would pervade the room: sweat, pizza, musk, and drugstore aftershave would be mixed together in there. Somewhat uninvited and slightly unwelcome, the doctor would just go on sitting there until something happened or nothing did. With another man in the room, Rafe would stop crying and collect himself. Rafe was devoted to benign authority: when sparring, he always bowed deeply and crisply and always walked away from his instructor backward. He had never gone through a rebellious, obnoxious phase and wouldn't start now.

The doctor would wait patiently with the young man, his son, who had fathered a child, "sired" one, that old strange verb that people now applied only to pedigreed dogs. Anyway, patience being one of his gifts, maybe the best of them, he would listen as his son lectured him on progressive politics and tae kwon do and werewolf fiction, his three great passions, as he recovered his composure. Donna, the boy's girlfriend, was in fourth place when it came to the passions, although the boy did not yet realize where she stood in his hierarchies. Only his father did. Poor thing, she would disappear eventually. They would all get over this.

Elijah's wife had written a story with Jupie in it. She had always had ambitions as a writer and had joined a downtown writers' organization called Scriveners' Ink, where she attended a workshop once a week led by a young woman, a recent MFA graduate.

Susan had shyly shown the story, entitled "Like Father Unlike Son," to her husband. In the story she had written, there is a young woman whose boyfriend is a sweet-tempered but infatuated adolescent male dupe. The girlfriend leads him around from one political meeting to another. The story is narrated by the boy's mother, who is not afraid to label her athlete son (a football player) to his face as "pussy-whipped"—the accusation is meant in good fun. The boy's father, a balding and overweight criminal lawyer given to pronouncements, provides comic relief and a regular income but somehow is not sufficiently supportive of his wife emotionally. He's too wrapped up in his work, it seems. Near the end of the story, as he crosses the street near his office, he is struck down by a Prius driven by an angry former client named Nancy, seeking revenge. This melodramatic touch at the story's climax leaves the boy's mother and the boy alone together, with the girlfriend, named Venus, now out of the picture, or forgotten, following the lawyer's painful death from internal bleeding. Together, in the story's last paragraph, the boy and his mother engage in troubled speculation about their future.

Elijah had rather liked the story. He didn't mind being killed off in it. He had complimented Susan on the narrative momentum, and he felt flattered that she would think of putting him into a piece of writing. In the story, the lawyer's name was Gerald, and Elijah had started to think of himself that way from time to time, not as himself but as Gerald, a disputatious character who turned up in his consciousness and his voice whenever he, Elijah, was driving, or arguing with insurance companies over billing practices.

One night two weeks later, with snack-food salt and cooking grease once more on his lips and fingers, the Jones Diet Plan having failed him again, the doctor arrived home to find Susan and Rafe sitting in the living room, waiting for him. They were both on the sofa, and because they weren't reading or watching TV or listening to music, he knew something was up.

"So?" he asked, as soon as he'd hung up his overcoat.

"Hey, Dad," Rafe said. His tousled curly brown hair framed his face, under the standing lamp, and his broad shoulders cast a shadow across the upholstery. He was barefoot. He didn't like to wear shoes or socks indoors and said that Asians had it right. With studied politeness, he said, "How was your day?"

How to describe a day that included a parade of sick kids and their parents, diagnoses, written prescriptions, and a trip to the hospital? "Oh, fine," he said. "Yours?"

"There's a thing," Susan said. "There's a thing that's come up, Eli."

"Yes? What thing would this be?" He waited. "Where's Theresa?" This was Rafe's sister.

"Upstairs." At that, both Rafe and his mother started speaking at once. They didn't seem to notice that they were talking simultaneously, or if they *did* notice, neither could stop to let the other one explain. They continued to talk over each other, although both of them were making the same point.

This simultaneous duo-outburst bothered the doctor even as he was listening to it. He knew his wife had a streak of self-absorption, a very little one, though still within normal range. Sometimes when other people were talking, she would excitedly interrupt as if no one else were in the room, as if no one else had ever existed. But to see Rafe talking over his mother—not even trying to outspeak her competitively, which would suggest that he knew she was there in the room with him, but calmly conversing with his father, as if the two of them were alone together—made Elijah feel a little sliver of despair.

The gist of their talk was that Donna's parents wanted to meet with Elijah—just with him, and no one else. They had made this request to their daughter, and she had passed it on to Rafe, who had passed it on to his mother. Now, here it was. Why hadn't they called *him*? At the office? He would have returned their call! Well, they just hadn't. Nor had they explained their rationale, or what the conversation would be about.

They wanted him to visit them late Sunday afternoon. *This* Sunday. In three days. Around five p.m. Given the Minnesota late autumn, the skies would be darkening by then. They lived in Delano, a semirural town west of Minneapolis. They were looking forward to talking to him, Susan said. They also planned, she told him, to give him some Christmas cookies, though it was still November.

When the doctor agreed, Rafe said he would text Donna, who would then tell her parents that his father would be coming. The most simple encounters could be made complicated with just a bit of effort. Rafe gave his father the address of Donna's parents, out in Delano.

That Sunday, the doctor pulled into their driveway with the aid of his car's GPS system. The family name, Lundgren, was attached with red metal letters to the driveway's mailbox. From the outside, the house itself projected an eerie normality, a rigidly resolute cheerfulness. A two-story colonial, it seemed to be projecting tremendous quantities of light from each window, as if every lamp and overhead fixture had been turned on to counter some terrible visitation, which was himself. The light was not just incandescent but somehow inflammatory, as if the walls and knickknacks were giving off a fiery plume that extended out onto the lawn, with its flecks of snow. The doctor shook his head to free himself from drowsiness and then groaned as he turned off the car's engine, opened the door, and heaved himself out, shaking off potato chip particles from his overcoat.

When he pressed the doorbell, he heard from inside the house a chime that sounded like the first few notes of "Onward, Christian Soldiers." When the door opened, he saw Donna's parents, both approximately his own age, somberly smiling in greeting as they ushered him in. Donna's mother held a plate of cookies, which she transferred to one hand as she waved him inside and shouted her greetings. Elijah was used to talking to parents about their children in his medical practice. He knew all the parental styles. Although he felt he was ready for any variety of family drama, he had forgotten how country people like the Lundgrens hooted in loud welcome for social occasions even when they weren't glad to see you. Noisy hospitality of this kind could be cold and heartless. The whole point was to avoid any trace of intimacy. In the Midwest, you just had to get used to it.

Mrs. Lundgren, neither pretty nor beautiful but solid, wore her brown hair in a moderately ostentatious beehive. Her eyes looked out from behind glasses attached to a tiny chain around her neck. Her shapeless skirt, a dull gray, gave the impression of formality heightened by the cameo brooch she wore on her blouse. She reminded the doctor of a loan officer he had once known at a bank, a no-nonsense woman whose face, after much experience of the world and probably much practice, radiated aggressive neutrality, seasoned with a bit of distaste for humanity.

Mr. Lundgren wore jeans and a sweater. His eyes were the impossibly deep blue that had so frightened the Native Americans when they gazed for the first time at the conquistadors. He shook hands with the doctor with a machinelike pneumatic grip, which out here signified masculine force and solidarity. "Hello," the host said, showing his teeth briefly, in what might have been a smile.

Donna's mother grinned at the doctor and directed him toward a living room chair planted in front of an audio speaker. Nearby was a side table with Ritz crackers topped with whipped cheese-colored goo. Each cracker had been placed carefully on a tiny paper napkin on which were printed minuscule blue flowers. A giant flat-screen TV, as large and solemn as an altar, held pride of place in front of the window, blocking the view. The TV's screen was dark, but music from *The Nut-*

*cracker* suite poured out from the speakers, making it hard to hear anything else over the Dance of the Sugar Plum Fairy. The doctor thought he heard Mrs. Lundgren shout out her own name, Eleanor, over the music, and she gestured at her husband and instructed the doctor to call him Herb. "We're Eleanor and Herb!" she said brightly, with an icy hostile smile. "Nice to meet you! Thanks for coming!" Without a rising inflection, she asked, "Can we get you a glass of water!" The doctor shook his head. He wanted whiskey and crusty bread, but you wouldn't get that in this household even if you begged for it on your knees.

He felt another moment of sleepiness.

Across the room, Herb Lundgren, slumped majestically in his La-Z-Boy chair, stared at the doctor impolitely. There was a clear division of labor in this marriage: talking would be Mrs. Lundgren's job, while her husband examined the guest for visual clues.

"I wonder," Elijah said, "if you could turn the music down? I can't quite hear you."

"Of course," Mrs. Lundgren said, advancing toward the audio system and fiddling with the dial. The sound dropped to a nearly inaudible hush, like an orchestra of mice playing inside the walls.

Mrs. Lundgren remarked on the weather, how cold it was getting. Her church, she said, worried about the homeless at this time of year. While she talked, the doctor surveyed the opposite wall above the sofa, where the Lundgrens had hung a cross-stitched *Last Supper*. Looking closer, the doctor suspected that the piece had been made from a mail-order hobby kit. Hours had been spent putting it together, in mad devotion. The mouse orchestra inside the walls continued to play Tchaikovsky while the doctor nodded in agreement to something Mrs. Lundgren had said that he actually hadn't quite heard. Over in the corner, on a bookshelf, was the *Oxford English Dictionary*. What was *that* doing here? Talk about clues: you must never underestimate your opponent. Someone here did a lot of reading.

Now Mrs. Lundgren was talking about Somali refugees, and the terrible conditions in the Sudan, and the shocking treatment of women in sub-Saharan Africa, clitoridectomies and the like. "And that's not the half of it," she said. The doctor nodded. "It makes you wonder sometimes about those people, how they think," she continued, as the doctor squirmed and closed his mouth, through which, he realized with embarrassment, he had been breathing. "We've been there, after all," she said. "We saw it with our very own eyes. We worked in a refugee camp. We know what we're talking about, so."

"Where was this?"

"The Kiziba refugee camp in Rwanda! Very inspiring!"

Mr. Lundgren glumly shook his head while he studied his hands. "But very hard work," he muttered.

Very hard, his wife repeated, but God expects us, she said, to help take care of the less fortunate, didn't the doctor agree? He did. Time passed. Global troubles were mentioned and disappeared into the conversational haze as if they were items of gossip. Suddenly the doctor remembered something his son had told him: Donna's mother worked as a middle school world history teacher. As teachers do, she continued to drone on: they, the Lundgrens, had tried to give all their extra money away to the poor for the sake of justice, and they had assembled a little scrapbook with photographs of children whom they had sponsored. "It's over there. We could show it to you. You can't go into heaven carrying bags of money!" Mrs. Lundgren said, shaking her head and laughing mirthlessly over the comic irony of it all. Every life was sacred, she said, didn't he agree? You *could* walk into heaven accompanied by the souls to whom you had lent a helping hand. *That* was possible. He that dwelleth in the secret place of the most High shall abide under the shadow of the Almighty, she said, confabulating.

No wonder Jupie had turned out the way she had.

The doctor rose to his feet and approached the plate of cookies, taking three for himself. Rarely in his life had he felt so hungry or so sleepy. He was starving in every possible way. He needed a nap, right now, and his hunger felt like an embrace of emptiness hugging him pitilessly, stifling him. His hunger, he suddenly thought, was *empirical*. In his mind arose an image of a man drinking a six-pack of air, one empty bottle after another. In rapid succession he ate the cookies and took three more, while Mrs. Lundgren lectured him on the holiness of all human existence and how existence was not a choice but a gift. Well, at least he knew where this was going. The lowest and highest hold the same rank in God's eyes, she was saying, tapping her finger on her knee. Of all the democrats, God was the greatest democrat. Status meant nothing to Him. He cared nothing for trinkets or the glittering machines of success. Before Him, we are all the same. The doctor felt himself growing impatient at all this moralizing and its transparent intentions. Everything she said sounded like a practiced speech, prepared and canned, like tomatoes in the basement. What did he, the doctor, think would save him?

"Excuse me?"

"Well, we were wondering, what will you do to be saved?" She leaned back and smiled. "We were wondering about that." She reached over for a Ritz cracker and popped it into her mouth. The doctor watched her chew. She ate like a peasant.

"Isn't that a very private matter?"

"Yes, it is," Mrs. Lundgren said, keeping her gaze on him, and suddenly he knew whom she resembled in both appearance and manner: Margaret Thatcher. "But you are the father of the young man who caused our daughter to become pregnant, aren't you? We wondered what values you had instilled in him. It may be a private matter, but it's ours now. Our matter."

"It's a father's job to instill values," Mr. Lundgren said, from his corner. "That's what a man does, so."

"I have tried to teach him to love the world," Elijah said. "And to treat everyone with respect. And to fight for what is right."

"Well, that's not enough," Mrs. Lundgren said, and the doctor intuited that she was a skilled tactician in argumentation and probably coached the high school debate squad. "If the world were enough, being worldly would be a virtue, wouldn't it? But it isn't. Does the world include our grandchild, yours and ours, the one who died?"

"You should take this up with your daughter," the doctor said.

"But we have," she told him. "And she seems to have been converted by your son. Converted to oblivion."

"Don't lecture me." The doctor spoke, but it was Gerald who had spoken up. Elijah seemed to be turning into his wife's fictional creation. Okay, fine.

"I'm *not* lecturing you. We're just asking questions and offering an opinion. We want to know what sort of man you are. As if we were all family here. Which we sort of are. Whatever *did* you teach Raphael? If I may ask?"

"Well," the doctor said, "first of all, we're not a family. What I taught Raphael, that's my business. And as for what I am, I'm a pediatrician."

"Yes, we know that. That's what you *do*. You care for children, which is quite admirable. But I asked you what you *are*."

"By what right do you ask me such a question?"

A rather long air pocket of dead silence followed, accompanied by the music. The doctor had never heard such a silence, with music in it.

Finally Mrs. Lundgren said, "The right of one parent to another. We have blood on our hands. All of us. And our children have blood on *their* hands. They have snuffed out a life, those two. They have caused suffering."

"Oh, for shit's sake," Gerald blurted out. "A woman has a right to choose. We all know that." Neither Lundgren flinched, as he had hoped they would. "I have to leave now."

"I don't think so," Mr. Lundgren said, and the doctor felt a chill.

"Do you think the happy choices of our children should depend on the suffering of fetuses? Is that the ticket? Is that the ticket to the universe? To its meaning? You should read your Dostoyevsky," Mrs. Lundgren said, a mild frenzy in her voice. "Don't you think a father should protect his infants and not kill them?"

"That's enough," the doctor said, standing up, although all he did was to reach for more cookies. Dostoyevsky in Delano! Of all things.

"You opened a jar," Mrs. Lundgren said. "The jar was full of pain. It was your jar."

He felt the room constricting and growing hot, warmed up from its already overheated condition. He felt Gerald overtaking him. It was Gerald who blurted out, "With all due respect, fuck you, ma'am, and you, sir, and good night."

She laughed, and for a moment the doctor felt himself admiring her. "What a silly person you are," she said. "Obscenity is *not* an argument. It is weak-minded. I had thought you would be more thoughtful. After all, you have a medical degree. You have not thought any of this through, not *any* of it, I can see that now. How shallow is the pool in which you swim. You are therefore self-deluded, cruel, and mean-spirited. I'm sorry to be so blunt, but we are in pain. Isn't it ironic? Your name being Elijah? And you, a doctor?"

"Now you're name-calling. I'm not a monster, and neither is my son. Perhaps *you* are the monster. It's time for me to leave now. Time to go."

"Is it time?" She glanced theatrically at her watch. "Perhaps I *am* a monster. But if I am, I'm a monster in the right army, and you're in the wrong one." She was still smiling eerily at him. The smile, fixed and meaningless, appeared to be surgically applied. Inside the walls of the house, the mice, perhaps on a salary, continued to play *The Nutcracker.* "The doctor is too busy to give us more than a few minutes of his precious time. So we must bid him farewell, Herb." She turned toward her husband, who seemed to have been mummified in his La-Z-Boy chair.

Who was Herb? It was only at this moment that Elijah realized he had already forgotten the first names of the Lundgrens. They *had* introduced themselves, what seemed like years ago, but their first names had not stuck. He put on his hat and coat, which had been draped over the newel post, and without another word, walked out to his cold car, thinking that never in his entire life had he had a social encounter like this one, nor would he ever again.

The stars had a spectral clarity in the moonless sky; no wonder people thought of them as the lights emanating from the dead. Shaken, hungry, and sleepy, the doctor took several random right turns until he finally found himself where he wanted to be: on a dirt road between fallow fields with hardly a house in sight. He wanted to be lost, and he was. He turned on the car's radio and turned it off again after hearing a few bars of atonal orchestral music. On the passenger seat rested a bag of Oreos, a box of Goldfish crackers, Cheetos, and Funyuns.

Rafe had trained in tae kwon do from the time he was a child. He had begged for lessons starting in second grade. The last time the doctor had seen Rafe sparring, the boy jumped so high that his father was startled; Rafe's moves were perfectly coordinated, and his flexibility seemed impossible. When he did a front rising kick, his extended foot was higher than his face. And fast. He dominated his opponent with a complicated series of kicks, and then he leaped out of range before his opponent could land anything on him. He never retreated. Why was the doctor thinking of that particular match, now? The blank merciless expression on Mrs. Lundgren's face had reminded the doctor of his son's face in combat.

In the distance the doctor saw the blinking red light of a radio transmission tower.

When you got down to the heart of things, you found desolation. Even in the midst of joy, you would find it. But you would find joy everywhere too. His son took joy in combat and sometimes laughed in practice sessions. So complicated, the mixture of the two. The doctor reached for the Oreos and ate several. He had attained a new low, or was it a new high, in sleepiness. He felt like fighting the drowsiness, but the drowsiness welcomed him, as any narcotic does, taking him up and away.

Christmas is coming, the doctor thought, the geese are getting fat. A child's rhyme from elementary school. Please put a penny in the old man's hat. *Why* are the geese fat? Who feeds the geese? If you haven't got a penny ... what will do ... the doctor heard a sound, without definition, and the road tilted a bit ...

Then things were flying around him—the cell phone had escaped from his coat pocket and was airborne in front of him, as were various other items, including the bags of snack food and a clipboard from the front seat—and he heard the sound of crunching or of some huge animal chewing up the car as it rotated and fell down into a ditch, and Elijah, now thoroughly awake, felt his driver's-side door open (how had *that* happened?), and he was ejected sideways, having forgotten to buckle his seat belt. *Narcolepsy,* he thought, with an odd diagnostic lucidity even as he came to rest on a little hill at the side of a field with, he instantly knew from the pain, a broken leg, a fractured tibia. He had always been a crack diagnostician, and even now on his back in the dirt, staring up at the night sky, cookie crumbs on his lips, his skills had not deserted him. *How stupid pain is.* From below the knee, thanks to the fracture, pain sent its dull, insistent message upstairs to the brain. Pain was like a siren. Pleasure never worked that way. The air had turned very cold.

Now he felt himself shivering rather violently from the cold and shock amid the field's dirt and snow. He saw the constellations above him wheeling in their eternal rounds, and a great peacefulness took hold of him, like the slow spreading of pleasure under the skin in a vague fog diffusing itself in a warm glow—a fog that lit up the soul. Underneath the peacefulness dwelt the pain. They *could* coexist.

He sniffed. The temperature was below freezing. He would die of hypothermia out here. No one would see him. He had landed in the middle of nowhere. His right hand was lacerated and was bleeding steadily. But it was perfectly all right, all of it, especially the bleeding.

The image of his son sparring intervened, and he realized that he didn't want the last faces he ever saw on Earth to be the faces of Herb and Eleanor Lundgren. Yes! He had remembered their names! He tried to sit up, and he looked around: in the distance, across the field directly behind him, stood a farmhouse with a single light at the top of a pole illuminating its driveway. He would have to be Gerald, it seemed, to get over there, and he could do it, and he thanked his wife for imagining Gerald, a combative man, into existence. He began crawling, using his elbows and dragging the rest of his incapacitated body, and he distracted himself from his own loud cries by admiring the sky full of stars indifferent to his situation, and also admiring the plainspoken stupidity of pain burning a hole in his leg. He crawled a certain distance, he didn't know how far, trying to reduce his cries to groans. What was the point in groaning? No one would hear.

He was in terrible pain but a rather good mood.

Ahead of him, in the field, to the right, out of the cold, out of the dark, out of the emptiness, a bell rang: his cell phone.

He crawled toward it. He dragged along the ground every cell of his corpulent body. By the time he reached the phone, the screen read, "Missed Call." The phone had been flung, as he himself had been, from the car, and now here it was, a gift from the gods who perhaps did not want him dead after all or had changed their minds, and after grasping the phone and reading the missed-call message—it had been from Democratic Party headquarters, no doubt soliciting a donation— he called home and told Susan what had happened to him and that he loved her, as she cried and shouted and then at last calmed down and told him how much she loved him and always had. Where was he? she demanded. He said he didn't know and would call the police. He promised to call her back, and then, peering down at the numbers, he called 911. He tried to describe his location to the dispatcher, but he didn't know the name of the road he had been on, so, between the bursts of imbecilic pain, he did his best to inform her about everything he saw, the blank landscape, the nondescript trees, the constellations above him (he was in shock, he knew), and again luck was with him: he said he thought he could maybe spot a tattered sign in the distance advertising a U-pick apple orchard, and the dispatcher said, oh, all right, yes, she knew where he was, and besides, they could find him using his phone and a GPS track. Stay calm, she told him. Don't move.

He disobeyed her. When the EMT guys arrived, their incandescent spotlight found his face, and he waved his arm at them and shouted for his life.

*In memory of THB*
*and for Chris*

# Vanity

He had stuffed his suitcase into the empty overhead bin, having purchased early-boarding rights from the airline, and had settled into his nonreclining seat, 32-B, when he had to stand up again to let the passenger in 32-A get past him. 32-A accompanied almost every move—taking off his raincoat, placing his crossword-puzzle book on the seat—with an unpleasant, guttural grunt. 32-A was a short man, of a certain age, stooped but solid, with hair dyed inky black. Apparently indifferent to mere appearances, he displayed traces of dandruff on his rumpled suit. Dandruff had also made its way onto his soiled and unpressed lime-green necktie. Harry Albert, who, by contrast, dressed rather elegantly and could still turn heads for his handsomeness, gave the man a nod, but 32-A did not nod in return. When 32-A finally sat down, he said, "Whoof."

Harry nodded and, between staged laughs, said, "That's right!" trying to be friendly. However, 32-A did not seem interested in Harry's amiable agreement and pulled out a battered copy of that day's Minneapolis *Star Tribune*. He turned to the business page and commenced to read. From time to time he uttered subvocalizations. Grim-faced, the flight attendants announced that they had "a very full flight." They proceeded to help passengers force their luggage into the already crammed overhead spaces. They gave instructions in the use of seat belts and oxygen masks, and eventually the plane was airborne.

Going through the cloud cover, the plane bounced and rattled. A few passengers laughed nervously. One overhead compartment popped open. A little girl screamed. The captain announced that there would be no beverage service, for now: too much turbulence.

"Bumpy flight," Harry Albert said.

"Unhrh," 32-A replied.

Well, he wouldn't bother to introduce himself to a man whose only conversational gambit consisted of nonverbal animal-like rumbling. Trying to doze, Harry heard 32-A making more peculiar sounds, like a dog having a nightmare. It would be impossible to doze off with this guy growling next to him. Feeling despondent, Harry reached for his paperback copy of *Schindler's List,* which someone had recommended.

32-A glanced over and grunted again. Finally he spoke up. "I was one of those." He had traces of a middle European accent, nearly gone, mostly dead but still living, a ghoul-accent.

"One of what?" Harry asked.

"I was a Schindler Jew," 32-A said.

Harry Albert felt a slight electrical shock. "I'm honored to meet you, sir," he said. He held out his hand and introduced himself to the man, who replied with his own name, "David Lowie." Or at least it sounded like Lowie. Harry didn't think it would be polite to ask 32-A (or, no: a person shouldn't think of a Holocaust survivor as 32-A) to repeat his name, so he refrained. Nor could he address his seatmate as David, presuming on an intimacy that did not exist. Mr. Lowie? Well, for the duration of an airplane flight, who needs names? Anonymity was the rule.

Apparently his seatmate didn't think so. "Harry Albert?" the man asked. "What's your last name?"

"It's Albert."

"Rrrgggr," the man replied dismissively. "That's an English name. But it sounds like a first name. Ha ha ha rrrgh." He coughed into a stickily soiled handkerchief, crusted with dried extrusions.

"Yes," Harry said, as the plane bounced around. A woman one row in front of him, on the other side of the aisle, was anxiously reading while holding her husband's hand. Okay: it was a turbulent flight but not life-threatening. "Could I ask you," Harry said, turning to his seatmate, "what Schindler was like? Did you ever talk to him?"

"*Talk* to him? What a question. No! Never. Don't be nuts. You didn't even *look* at him."

"You didn't look at him?"

"Of course not. I kept my head down. I could hardly tell you what he looked like. You didn't look at *any* of the Germans. If you were smart."

"Why not?"

"Why not? I see you don't— Well, *because*. It's, um. Because obviously. Because you didn't look at them, Schindler included. Not any of them. You know, I was going to be in that movie. Spielberg, that *fellow*, not a tall man, flew me to the grave site. In Jerusalem! With the camera set up, shooting, take one take two, I put a stone on the grave, me. Filmed. Lights, camera, action."

"Were you—?"

"I got a good dry-cleaning business in Milwaukee," the man said. "Several stores. Successful! A new one out in Brookfield, maybe one in Waukesha. We're looking into it. My life doesn't depend on being in a Hollywood film. I got left on the floor."

"I'm sorry?"

"I got left on the floor. What's the matter? This phrase, you never heard it? When they cut you out?"

"Oh," Harry said, "the *cutting-room floor*. You got left on the cutting-room floor."

"This is what I said."

"No, you said you got left on the floor. I'm sorry. I didn't know what floor you were talking about."

"What'd you think I was talking about? The second floor, lingerie, where you buy ladies' undergarments? This is— Well, you're a kid, no wonder you don't know anything. So. I went over there, a nice hotel, free food, the Holy Land, Jerusalem, he shoots me, I am directed, but where am I in the film? Nowhere. Not that I *mind*."

"I'm sorry. You should have been in it."

"You're telling me. They flew me to Jerusalem. Coddled, there and back. A seat in first class both ways. So tell me. They don't want me in their film. What's wrong with me? My appearance? *Anything?* No. I don't think so."

Harry looked more carefully at his seatmate's face, which was of a formidable ugliness. Of course, ugliness was no one's fault despite what Oscar Wilde had said about the matter. Lowie's elderly expression was one of sour, downturned-mouth disgust mixed with a very precise rudeness. However, he was a survivor, so hats off.

"You see anything wrong with my face?" The man was persistent.

"Not a thing," Harry Albert said. "Clearly they made a mistake, leaving me on the floor. I mean you. Not me. *You.* Slip of the tongue."

"You, they *didn't* leave on the floor. With your looks, a handsome English prince like yourself, they never leave you down there. Guys like you? *Always* in the movie, upstairs, presidential suite, the best treatment, silk sheets. Palace guard out in front, beefeaters, room service. You, they put in the golden carriage. *Horses* pull you. People waving, want your autograph. Guys like me, never, unless we fight for it, compete, in a free market. How come therefore they fly me to Jerusalem if they're only going to waste my time? This remains a puzzle. Even my wife can't solve it. So why are you flying to Vegas?"

"A business conference," Harry Albert said.

"What do you do?"

"Manufacturer's rep. Medical devices."

"Well, good. That's a good business. The economy can *never* hurt you if you sell to sick people. The sick are always with us, I assure you, Harry Albert. Always will be. A full supply of the sick. *Hoards* of sick. More of them always, too, including the old, like, what do the kids call them, zombies."

"And you?"

"What about me?"

"What're you going to be doing in Vegas?"

"Oh. Me? I'm meeting my wife. She got there yesterday, a cheaper flight, one night on her own, and she's been playing the slots. I had work I had to do, talk to a banker here in Minneapolis, therefore I'm leaving today. She's been playing the slots, did I mention that? And tonight and tomorrow and the next day, we're going to the shows. The shows in Las Vegas are the best in the world! The nightlife. It's— Am I explaining? Even a child knows. Do you like nightlife?"

Harry Albert liked nightlife very much but suddenly felt that a certain tact might be necessary. "Yes," he said.

"And the showgirls?"

"Showgirls? Meh," Harry Albert said.

"Meh?"

"Yeah, meh. I like the costumes sometimes," Harry Albert said.

"Costumes, yes, sequins and glitter, but they're not the point. What's with the 'meh,' if I may ask?"

"I can explain."

"This explanation I would like to hear. Every year, my wife and I go to Vegas. We have fun. We gamble a little, we go to the shows. Performances, by the very best: Wayne Newton, Olivia Newton-John, Sammy Davis Jr. Have you seen him? What a voice! Versatility! Perhaps he has no appeal to English royalty like Prince Albert, but what's the harm? Okay, so he's been dead for a while, but my point is: greatness. Also, and I don't think I mentioned this, the sun. The sun is a prizewinner. Have you ever seen rain in Las Vegas?"

"No. Never."

"Exactly. They're smart. They have the sun under contract."

"And rain?"

"Rain they don't employ."

"Well, it's a desert out there," Harry Albert said.

"Yes, but nightlife blooms where no rain falls. You've

heard that expression? What time is it at the blackjack table? Who cares? Shoot out the clocks! The showgirls, tanned and healthy, where do these girls come from? They pop up out of the cactus plants, could be. Do they have mothers? Are they desert creatures like armadillos? I don't bother to ask. Even my wife enjoys the showgirls, as long as they're dancing. I like to sit close, so you can see the sweat. Sweat drips down their long legs. I like that. Criticize me if you want to."

"Ah."

"You don't like them? Prince Albert, I believe you said you were indifferent to showgirls."

"Well, I'm gay."

"So are the girls. Everyone smiles in Vegas. Everyone is happy and carefree, except for the losers of life savings. You have to know when to stop. Common sense. I don't see the problem."

"You don't get it," Harry Albert said. "I'm queer."

The plane bounced, and 32-A sat back. "You're a queer?"

"Yup."

"You don't look like it. What's the *point* in that? Please explain."

"Excuse me?"

"Why would anyone want such a thing? No showgirls for you? Just showboys? With nice hair? Tap dancers? Playing the gold piano?"

"Could be."

The old man leaned back and puffed out his cheeks. "I've known people like you. And, let me say, I am open-minded. Every hedgehog has a law for itself, hedgehog law. For me, however, queer has no appeal. Your particular kingdom is closed to me. So, you get to Vegas, no showgirls, no pretty waitresses, what *have* you got?"

"Plenty," Harry Albert said.

"Please don't describe. A cute smile I suppose can be anywhere. But okay. Prince, listen to me. Like I said, *open-minded* is my motto. You got your book there, you're reading about Schindler, but this is America now, different hedgehog laws. So, okay, what am I—? I'm saying, and this is very simple, so listen. These other people on the plane, screaming now, turbulence, they would say it too if they only stopped screaming. Which is: enjoy life. In your hedgehog royalty way."

"Thank you," Harry Albert said. "Trust me. I do enjoy it."

"You're kind of solid-looking. You don't look delicate, if I may say. Or *sensitive*, even, which, I might as well tell you, I despise. *Feelings?* No, not for me."

"I work out."

"You work out what?"

"In the gym. Circuit training. Also, I box. I'm a fighter." Harry Albert made a fist, and the old man nodded. "I have a good punch."

"That's right. You must. That's *right*." The old man had become quite vehement. "So there's something I want you to do, Prince." The old man reached into his pocket and drew out a business card. On it had been printed his name, the name of his business, Go-Clean, with its website, and an e-mail address. He handed it to Harry Albert. "First we shake hands. Not every day do I meet a member of the English royal family trained in pugilism."

"But I'm not—"

The old man held up his hand. "Don't deny. You're thinking: this old man, he's crazy, a Schindler Jew, suffering has made him insane, and I'm telling you, no, it didn't. Maybe a joker." He held out his hand, and Harry Albert shook it. "A joker is what it made me. A joker vacationer. An American going on vacation to Las Vegas, where my wife already is, that's what I am. An American like you. So what *you* do is, you go to your business conference and then night falls, and you enjoy the nightlife in your hedgehog way with your hedgehog friends, and you write to me, you send me a note telling me you're okay. Because now we are friends. You said you are honored to meet me."

"Yes, I am."

"And I am likewise honored to meet you, English royalty. Freed at last from the palace, like *Roman Holiday*. Even though you don't look like Audrey Hepburn. Maybe more Oscar De La Hoya. Are you vain, like him?"

"Yes. But I'm not—"

"Like I said: don't bother to deny." The old man turned to gaze out the window. "We'll be landing soon. Where are the free peanuts? The free beverage?" He turned back to Harry Albert, and all at once a smile broke out on his profoundly ugly face, a transfixing smile. "This is a very annoying flight. Except for you. Prince, you're good company," he said. "You keep a person interested. Send me a letter. Tell me what it's like."

Sitting in his hotel room, satiated with pleasure, the other young man still in bed, prettily sleeping, Harry Albert opened his laptop and began to write.

*Dear David,* he wrote, *I promised that I would write to you and now I'm doing just that. I've had some lucky streaks in Las Vegas since I got here. The conference went well, I made some contacts, I met some people.* He glanced at the bed before turning back to the computer screen and the keyboard. *You could say I won.*

*Business in my field is good. I don't have to worry about money.*

For a moment he gazed out the open window at the lights of the city. He liked to keep the windows open with the curtains drawn back in case other visitors, in other hotels, happened to glance out, *Rear Window* style, in his direction. They would see him disporting himself in the company of others. Let them envy him. Let them envy his good looks, his luck.

*You asked me if I'm vain. And I sure am. I don't think about my looks too much, anyhow not much more than most people do, but it gets me results. When I get older, I'll have to drop it. My appearance will start to fail. But by then I'll be in love. I'm too busy for love right now. But by then, in the future, I won't care how pretty anybody is, and they won't care about my looks either, and we'll be fine.*

*The point is, I love my life. So do you. I was pleased and honored to meet you.*

*Thanks for the conversation.*

He signed the e-mail "Prince Albert."

A week later, back in Minneapolis, he received a reply, three words. *Don't kid yourself.*

The e-mail note was unsigned.

# CODA

# *Coda*

The Stone Arch Bridge crosses the Mississippi River between Father Hennepin Bluffs Park on the east bank and Mill Ruins Park on the west in the heart of Minneapolis, Minnesota. This bridge, which once supported railroad traffic in and out of the city, has twenty-one stone arch spans. Wikipedia tells us that James J. Hill, the Empire Builder, had the bridge constructed in 1883, and in the early 1990s it was converted to a pedestrian-and-bicycle bridge.

On warm days in late spring or summer, the bridge serves as a kind of promenade, or gallery, for pedestrians, and on such days you are likely to see both visitors and city dwellers walking across it with no particular destination in view. That obese man, for example, with rainbow suspenders, who is wearing a frown and a faraway look, and whose wife— they both have wedding rings—has her hand through his arm for support, might he be a doctor, a pediatrician? Close behind him is a woman mumbling to herself, and you might imagine that she's translating a poem in her head out of an Eastern European language into English. And on this side, speeding past you, are two people on bicycles, one of them looking vaguely Asian-American, the other, his girlfriend or wife (they pass by too quickly for the idle pedestrian to spot any evidence that they are married) smiling and happily shouting instructions in his direction.

Near Wilde Roast Café, a gay-themed restaurant on St. Anthony Main, you bump into a man who is texting on his iPhone, and you excuse yourself and continue on your way.

The day is beautiful: royal-blue skies, a light breeze, temperature in the high sixties, the sort of day that Sinclair Lewis, who once lived here, would mark in his journal as "p.d."—that is, a perfect day. These people are gathered here like the Sunday strollers in Seurat's painting *A Sunday Afternoon on the Island of La Grande Jatte,* where the beautiful laziness, the indolence of those out for a breath of air, offers itself as a glimpse of Paradise. Delmore Schwartz, obsessed with that painting, wrote these lines in his poem "Seurat's Sunday Afternoon Along the Seine":

> *The sunlight, the soaring trees and the Seine*
> *Are as a great net in which Seurat seeks to seize and hold*
> *All living being in a parade and promenade of mild, calm*
> *    happiness:*
> *The river, quivering, silver blue under the light's variety*
> *Is almost motionless.*

How I love that poem. But, after all, how much happiness can there be, without its opposite close by, so that we can know what happiness is?

Look: the pedestrians gaze over the bridge's side at the Falls of St. Anthony, the only falls anywhere on the Mississippi River. Who was St. Anthony, for whom these falls, and this part of the city, were originally named? A much-loved man, born in Lisbon as Fernando Martins, he became a Franciscan and took the name Anthony. Known for his preaching, he did not live long, dying at the age of thirty-five. Legend tells us that when his body was exhumed years after his death, his body was "found to be corrupted" (that is, it was dust), but his tongue was glistening and intact, thanks to the purity of his teachings.

Before Minneapolis was Minneapolis, it was St. Anthony Falls. St. Anthony is still known as the Saint of Lost Things, and even lapsed Catholics will sometimes repeat, "Dear Saint Anthony, please look around. Something is lost that must be found." He is also thought to restore lost tranquility, and in one such prayer, he is beseeched "to restore to me peace and tranquility of mind, the loss of which has afflicted me even more than my material loss." Father Hennepin, upon seeing these falls for the first time, described them as "astonishing in scope and power." But much doubt has been cast on his histories, and the histories themselves are considered unreliable. Present-day historians consider Father Hennepin to have been a prodigious liar.

But the day is beautiful, all the same.

# Acknowledgments

These stories had several early readers, and I especially want to thank Stephen Schwartz, Lorrie Moore, William Lychack, Robert Cohen, Eileen Pollack, and Louise Glück for their help. "Forbearance" is distantly based on an anecdote told by Miller Williams decades ago. My thanks to him and to Giuseppe Belli. Thank you to Kyle Kerr for the idea. As ever, my gratitude goes to Dan Frank and Liz Darhansoff.

BELIEVERS

The seven stories and novella in *Believers* introduce people who walk the razor's edge between despair and faith: the young woman with a sweetly nurturing boyfriend who may have a secret history of violence; the housewife whose upstairs neighbor is either a child-killer or a pathetic fabulist; the man trying to discover the truth about his father, a Catholic priest whose involvement with a sinister wealthy couple toppled him from grace. Perfectly modulated, unerringly seen, and written in prose of transparent beauty, *Believers* is storytelling at its finest.

Short Stories

HARMONY OF THE WORLD

In these ten stories, Charles Baxter shows his genius in making his characters' everyday sufferings seem utterly unprecedented, even as he reminds us, gently and with a sly comic twist, that everything they feel is only the collateral damage of being human. Whether he is writing about the players in a rickety bisexual love triangle or a woman visiting her husband in a nursing home, probing the psychic mainspring of an obsessive weight lifter or sifting through the layers of resentment, need, and pity in a friendship that has gone on a few decades too long, Baxter enchants us with the elegant balance of his prose and the unexpectedness of his insights. *Harmony of the World* is a masterpiece of lucidity and compassion.

Short Stories

ALSO AVAILABLE

*Feast of Love*
*Saul and Patsy*
*Through the Safety Net*

VINTAGE CONTEMPORARIES
Available wherever books are sold.
www.vintagebooks.com